Other Works By Larissa Shmailo

POETRY

Medusa's Country, MadHat Press, 2016

#specialcharacters, Unlikely Books, 2014

In Paran, BlazeVOX [books], 2009

Fib Sequence (chapbook), Argotist Ebooks, 2011

A Cure for Suicide (chapbook), Červená Barva Press, 2006

FICTION

Patient Women, BlazeVOX [books], 2015

TRANSLATION

Victory over the Sun by Alexei Kruchenych, Červená Barva Press 2014

Bibliography of Bible Translations in the Languages of the Russian Federation, Other Countries in the Commonwealth of Independent States, and the Baltic States, Eugene A. Nida Institute for Biblical Scholarship of the American Bible Society, 2011

ANTHOLOGY

Editor, *Twenty-first Century Russian Poetry*, Big Bridge Press, 2013

RECORDINGS (Digital and CDs)

Exorcism, SongCrew, 2009

The No-Net World, SongCrew, 2006

Sly Bang
Larissa Shmailo

Spuyten Duyvil
New York City

Excerpts from *Sly Bang* appeared in *Unlikely Stories 20th Anniversary Edition*, 2018.
"Vow," "For Six Months with You," "Jamas Volveré, "Lager NYC," and "How My Family Survived the Camps" appeared in *In Paran* by Larissa Shmailo.
"Your Probability Amplitude" appeared in *Plume* and *#specialcharacters* by Larissa Shmailo.
"*Schweinerei*" appeared in the *St. Petersburg Review* and *#specialcharacters* by Larissa Shmailo.
"Copy Cat" appeared in *Altered Scale* and *New Mirage Journal.*
The audio poetry "Warsaw Ghetto" is a track on the CD, *Exorcism*, and is available from iTunes and other digital distributors.

Thanks to Robin M. Mayer for invaluable assistance with this book.

ISBN 978-1-947980-98-3

Library of Congress Cataloging-in-Publication Data

Names: Shmailo, Larissa, author.
Title: Sly bang / Larissa Shmailo.
Description: New York City : Spuyten Duyvil, 2019.
Identifiers: LCCN 2018047697 | ISBN 9781947980983
Classification: LCC PS3619.H6258 S58 2019 | DDC 813/.6--dc23
LC record available at https://lccn.loc.gov/2018047697

Dedicated to every woman
killed in fiction because she had sex.

God bless the Poisson Distribution.

—Nora the fearless Jesuit

We discover NORA masturbating on an expensive leather couch in a railroad apartment on Manhattan's Upper West Side. The front door is barricaded by two chairs; a layer of broken glass covers the corridor to the main room. The apartment looks like someone has been smashing everything that can be smashed, which, in fact, Nora has been doing.

NORA finishes and pulls on a tight black jumpsuit and boots and twists her long dark hair into a bun held together by a lacquered chopstick with a pointed edge; it is a weapon. She looks like a voluptuous Diana Rigg from *The Avengers*, but sweatier and grittier. She is tired.

As the scene begins, we hear long, loud clanging tones from a mysterious source. They seem to be moving in a circle around Nora. Suddenly, they stop. NORA sits bolt upright. We hear a measured, friendly, distinct MALE VOICE, although there is no man in the room.

MALE VOICE: We give this training to our best operatives.

NORA lies back down; she is listening.

MALE VOICE: We give this training to our best operatives, Nora. Most of them crack up completely, take hatchets and hack up their wives, run screaming into the night or die, but you have passed with flying colors. Without even breaking a sweat.

NORA looks around the room. Dismissing the voice, she begins stretching on the couch in asana. She ends her routine by hanging head downward, legs propped on the couch, breathing slowly and deeply. The rhythmic clangs start again.

We now see what look like holographic images on the ceiling and walls. They are battle scenes from Kosovo, brutal rapes and dismemberments; military aircraft hover above the blackened air of the battleground. The pilots of the craft look happy and seem to be maneuvering for a better view of a gangbang of a naked brown girl with a burka pulled up around her head; the girl, who is about ten, is rationally requesting that her rapists kill her.

NORA shuts her eyes. The room is flooded by a barrage of messages. They order her to kill her mother and fuck her father. NORA picks up and palms a fragment of amethyst geode, running her fingers along the sharp purple crystals. She looks into a hole in the armrest of the couch. There is a miniature device there, a transmitter. Around the armrest, we see a row of Pellegrino water bottles, some with bases strategically broken, jagged, also suitable as weapons.

Refreshed from the yoga, NORA lies down, and despite the clangs, sleeps. The clangs intensify, now, louder and more rapid. NORA opens her eyes and yawns. She turns toward the central, loudest clang.

NORA: (YELLS OVER THE CLANGS) What is "organic," Deal? Do you remember your biochemistry, Doctor? Humans are organic, Deal. (SHAKES HER HEAD IN DISGUST). Can't have grad students cover your ass forever, Deal. (STANDS AND STRETCHES. BRAVELY, HIDING HER EXHAUSTION) Who's listening today, boys? Yes, you, Deal. How are the Mengele experiments on the Mexican orphans going?

The clangs stop for a moment. NORA sighs and turns her head into the armrest of the couch, trying to sleep again. As soon as she gets comfortable, the clangs start again, this time with a pronounced chalk-on-blackboard screech. NORA turns, seriously pissed.
NORA: Stand back, Deal, you small-dicked punk; I want to talk to your handlers. How is The Howard? Big man do big deals today? Ussasis, nice yacht; be careful one of the crew don't pitch you over on the rocks; could happen, you know. I do have friends (TURNS AS THOUGH TO ADDRESS SOMEONE ELSE). And how is my Rocky Horror boyfriend doing, Ouspensky? Dearest Genya, what's on the slab in the lab today? A three-year-old girl, probably; that is your preferred dating age. (LOOKS AROUND ROOM). I have gotten quite a few of you one-percenters pissed off lately, haven't I? So be it. Just remember, when you go to sleep, that all your billions can't stop the flow of blood from a carefully placed shiv to your neck. As I've said, I do have friends. (LAUGHS, A BLUFF) And you are not going to kill me. If you wanted to, you would have done it by now. You have something more, shall we say, interesting planned for me. (RETURNS TO COUCH, THROWS A BLANKET OVER HER HEAD. FROM UNDER BLANKET) You bore me.
CLANGS STOP.
We see NORA under the blanket. Her ear is over the hole in the armrest. The transmitter activates and emits a series of beeps. NORA shuts her eyes; she is truly exhausted and at breaking point. Suddenly, a voice that sounds like Johnny Depp's comes through the transmitter.
JOHNNY DEPP: Am I going too fast for you?

NORA smiles; she likes Johnny Depp and the voice seems helpful.
JOHNNY DEPP: (REPEATS) Am I going too fast for you?
NORA hears this simultaneously with four other sentences, or the fragments of sentences. She hears quotes from Shakespeare: *Shall I compare thee to a summer day?* Nietzsche: *What doesn't kill me makes me stronger*; the Beatles: *All you need is love.* The sounds emit in half-syllables, then a barrage of sememes. They are for the most part positive. She hears "Stand by Me," the *Ode to Joy*, "Soul Man," and the *1812 Overture*, a few bars or words all at once. NORA breathes easily and relaxes; this strange medley seems to be restorative. She leans into the device.
Now a kaleidoscope of images and sound bites flood her in a synesthesia of short-attention-span theater. She smells the seaweed of the Mediterranean and Lady Gaga's meat dress, but also her mother's voice and father's eyes. Her body shifts and twitches on the couch as though she is in the rapid-eye-movement state of sleep. The JOHNNY DEPP voice wails and ululates and keeps asking, "Am I going too fast for you?" The flood of sememes become hyper-Sanskrit in staccato: *aum chit anan* and the sound of a carousel and AC/DC singing "Highway to Hell."
NORA is now in a series of movie clips; she is Columbia in *The Rocky Horror Show* at a black-and-white Black Mass party given by Prince Eugene (Genya) Ouspensky; she is murdered by the *In Cold Blood* killers and immediately becomes Harper Lee nurse-maiding Capote as he ghoulishly awaits the killers' death. She is hugged by Gregory Peck in *To Kill a Mockingbird* and next is on a

plantation vomiting whatever root Scarlet O'Hara ate just before the intermission of *Gone with the Wind*. All of this takes about three minutes.
The psychic slideshow stops. NORA awakes, refreshed, and lifts the blanket from her face. She is smiling; she looks as though she has had a good night's sleep. A voice comes over the transmitter; it is Michael, a serial killer.
MICHAEL: Hey, there!
NORA jumps, startled by the sudden voice, then recognizes it. (MUTTERS) Today, I will judge nothing that happens.
MICHAEL: How do you like my tapping into your CIA transmitter? How did you like the REM sleep? You needed it pretty bad. Helpful, right? Pretty brilliant of me to develop a synthetic dreaming code, if I say so myself. Still think Prince Ouspensky is the smartest man in the world?
NORA: Hello, Michael. Are there walls between us, buildings, I hope?
MICHAEL Yes. And I've triple-locked the door and bound my feet in case I get the urge to kill you, to give you a little time. Oh, God, I shouldn't have said "kill you"—I have a hard-on the size of Uranus—oh, your anus—wait, I need to jerk off.
NORA: Okay, but think about the dead ones and not me.
MICHAEL: I came; you should see the ejaculate, it would impress you. See, I could just think about it and not have a kill in front of me. I'm getting better; soon I'll be able to come inside a real live girl. I have been trying. But you haven't said anything about my program. You liked it; my sensors picked that up. And you look almost human now. I really am a genius.

NORA: Are you planning a kill now, Michael? Do you have a girl with you? Is she alive? (PICKS UP A POLICE RADIO AND REPORTS): Volkhonsky. I have the whereabouts of the Jersey Skinner in Manhattan, Upper West Side in a radius of a mile from West 72nd Street. May have live victim with him. Uses the name Michael Distefano. Be on the lookout. Ten four.
MICHAEL: You know they will never find me, Nora. If you can't, those jerks never will. And I wouldn't be killing if you would abreact me.
NORA: I'm not a psychiatrist, Michael. Turn yourself in and we'll get you the best medical care possible.
MICHAEL: Only you can do it, Nora. I've seen you do it. That idiot Hudderman who stuffed all his kill into his mother's closet, you did it to him. He's normal now.
NORA: It will probably kill you. Let me do my thing. (PICKS UP CELL PHONE AND DIALS. INTO PHONE): Special Agent Volkhonsky. I have the Jersey Skinner on the Upper West Side, radius one mile from West 72nd Street. Goes by the name of Michael Distefano. Armed and extremely dangerous.
MICHAEL: (INTERRUPTING). Stop called those jerks. I get jealous.
NORA: I won't abreact you.
MICHAEL: Yes, you will. Eventually, you will. The schmuck I usually am needs to know about this stuff. Think about the terrified young girls I lure to my lair and do magnificent, unspeakable things to. Do it for them.
NORA FIGHTS RETCHING.
MICHAEL: Yes, I'm a monster. You have no idea. But you feel safe around me because you know I love you,

genuinely; I really do and it's a wonderful feeling. I've never felt this way before. Didn't I impose the rule of never being in the same building with you, don't I manacle myself and triple-lock the door? I really want to kill you and fuck your corpse, Nora, but I fight this absolutely overwhelming desire just in order to have your friendship. I've never had a friend before.
NORA: Michael, why are you so obsessed with me?
MICHAEL: You are the only person I know who cares about me, this personality, Michael.
NORA: I don't.
MICHAEL: You do. Don't tell me you don't, you do; I can sense it. Everyone loves the mediocrity that I am when I'm not Michael. He's broke and stupid and he has more friends than God. But me, everyone hates and fears me.
NORA: You like that. That's why you torture the girls.
MICHAEL: Not really. Their fear is irrelevant to me. I just need them dead for sex and to do my art. You are not like those vacuous cows; you're different. You give me hope. I never felt hope before you were assigned to my case. Hope, Nora, a very specific hope.
NORA PUTS IN ANOTHER POLICE REPORT. MICHAEL IGNORES IT; THIS IS ROUTINE BETWEEN THEM.
MICHAEL: My name's not really Michael, I'd like to point out. Or Distefano. Michael was the name of your first boyfriend and Distefano was the name of your childhood friend. It's manipulative, I know, but all's fair, right? So, abreact me.
NORA: Under no circumstances will I abreact you. You will go berserk and God knows how many you will kill then. And you will die. Tell me your real name and

address. (FLIPS HER BODY FACE DOWN INTO THE PILLOW. MUTTERS.) Or undress. Address me and undress. Birdies, where are you? Help me. The clangs sound like you, like the cries of large metallic birds o god I told they heard …

"Nora, wake up!"

Michael wakes woke is waking her what's up wake up …

"You're dreaming. I administered a REM sleep code to you. You are still sleeping."

Disoriented and dizzy, Nora cased the room, holding herself erect on the back of a chair. Was she dreaming? Yes, no? What had just happened? The clangs? Silent but real; what else? The birds … stop. Michael.

"Where are you, Michael?" she asked groggily.

"At a safe distance," the transmitter replied. "And you could abreact me the same way. And I won't kill if I abreact. And I can take it. Then I can stop and you will forgive me all of it, won't you? I'll live on an island in Alaska so I can't kill you, even though I want to so badly, and you will forgive me and write to me. Right? You forgive the others when they stop. So, you will forgive even me." The first notes of the *Ode to Joy* rang out, then faded beautifully away.

Nora was fully awake. She had been dreaming, dreaming within a dream. She took the jagged amethyst geode into her hand and ran the edges along her fingers again. The house was a wreck and they were coming.

"Exactly, dear girl," Michael continued, business-like, "I'm not here to ask your help today; I'm here to help you, and you sorely need it—you look a mess, darling, and your mind is quite weakened, much more than you think. There is an army of serial killers, mad scientists, and ultrarich sociopaths after you."

Nora nodded. This was true and Michael might really be the only friend she had; she shuddered at the thought. She closed her eyes and lapsed back into dream. The echo of the clangs rang in her head. Deal. Fucking Deal.

"You draw serial killers to you like flies to honey," Deal had observed during one of Nora's psychotherapy sessions. "Yet, they don't kill you."

"Serials have wives and children," Nora responded. "They don't kill them; they can even be affectionate with them. Like a mobster with a Madonna-wife and mistress-whore complex. You should know; you break down women that way, too."

"No," Deal shook his fat round head. "No, Nora—you are the cure. The cure for serial psychopathy for sure, maybe even sociopathy itself."

"Maybe you should be curing my PTSD."

"You don't have PTSD. And you weren't incested or abused, and you are not a multiple personality. You're just a girl who likes to fuck. Read the literature of the False Memory Foundation I gave you. Reputations are being ruined by your crap."

And Deal, incester and charter member of the False Memory Foundation, would love to be known as the great medical mind that had cured sociopathy, incurable to date. Even Alcoholics Anonymous spoke of the intractable, the constitutionally incapable, incapable of being honest. Unfortunates, the program called them, but, nonetheless, hopeless. Deal would use Nora's brain waves or pheromones or urine to cure the Mafiosi and senators and gang members and ordinary cubicle backstabbers who knew wrong from right and didn't give a shit, unlike psychopaths like Michael who did not, who were truly insane.

Maybe Deal was right: the weirdest and most murderous elements on the planet instinctively sought her out—and kept her alive. Even the ubernarcissistic serial rapist and cannibal Bost did. Except now she had pissed him off by telling him that Ouspensky was smarter than him. Bost considered himself the only intelligent man on the planet, but all the men she knew seemed to believe that about themselves. But even now, even in a jealous rage, even Bost might not cannibalize her, she reflected. They all, strangely, did not harm her.

But there were limits and she was busting them right and left, if anyone was listening. She had the goods on them. And they were coming for her: Deal wanted her brain for experiments and Ouspensky, sick mad scientist and most perverted man on the planet—and the love of her life—who knew what *he* wanted?

Nora looked about the room. She sensed she was safe from Michael. And she would probably be able to hold off the other serials and get out of the apartment somehow. Now, especially now, it was essential she survive.

Where to go? China. Get brown contact lenses; with her high cheekbones and fine dark hair, she could pass for Asian except for her round blue eyes. A factory worker in Guangdong, until she could regroup and find allies. Scarce now, those.

She looked at the fragments of glass and metal around the room. None of this would be any use against a gun, but the worst perps did not want her dead, she knew that; they had something more horrible planned. She had stopped thinking a while ago and was now just trying to put space between her reactions and her responses to the stimuli of each day. A knee-jerk response could be fatal.

Michael interrupted her reverie, miffed. "Nora, where are you? You are not paying attention."

"And you hate it when women don't pay attention to you, don't you, Michael?"

Nora could feel Michael's supercilious sneer. "I don't give a rat's ass about women, Nora. I like corpses with vaginas."

Nora and Audrey Uhuru, the agency's best profiler and one of the best detectives in the nation, had worked together on the Jersey Skinner case. "Michael Distefano" was likely a true multiple personality, split sharply in two, Norman-Bates style. From the kills they had carefully examined they postulated that one of Michael's alters was a kind and sweet New Jersey man, likely a photographer. But this personality's alter ego was a dissociated and flagrantly mad serial killer who skinned his victims alive and turned them into preternaturally lifelike dolls. Michael's day-to-day life was probably unremarkable, a series of wedding portraits and Bat Mitzvahs. But Michael's other personality, which the sweet mediocrity was completely unaware of, was a predator of astonishing proportions, with, Nora suspected, thousands—what am I saying, she thought: *thousands!*—of kills to his name. He was a living, breathing, one-man atrocity.

She lay down and put her head on the armrest. A jolt of a human presence inside rocked her. Michael laughed. "Let me show you that I know all your secrets, Nora, dear," he boasted. "Watch!"

There they were, Nora's most cherished and important secrets.

"No!" Nora shook the invading presence out of her soul but saw that it was too late. He had somehow come into her deep, dreaming mind and seen them, the great birds, the aliens, the huge swanlike pterodactyls who sang to her in the midst of all the mindfuck clutter.

She was getting a pedicure, before all the shit had hit the fan, and a tall woman with exceptionally good plastic surgery on her neck and face sat down in the chair next to her and took off her enormous shoes. Nora stared at the huge feet with the talon-like nails —no, not talon-like: they *were* talons, large and yellow and curled like fishhooks. And the vein structure, thick and purple, boilingly vivid against the yellow skin, was like nothing she had ever seen before, even after booking the most weathered and drug-deformed perps on Earth.

The tiny head turned and smiled. The tiny hands, with the most perfect pink nails she had ever seen, waved, put her shoes back on, dropped three hundred dollars in the confused manicurist's hands, and left.

Nora ran home in excitement. Contact. It was first contact. And it felt as God-glorious wondrous as ever she thought it would.

And Michael, catching her tired and off-guard, had somehow seen this in her mind. She stopped herself. That was ridiculous. He must have overheard her mutter in her sleep. Damn! Who else had heard?

"No, my dear, you did not mutter in your sleep." Michael was very pleased with himself. "You see, I know you—admit that you like the fact that at least one man does." Michael's voice dropped to a whisper. "I know about the aliens, know about the great pterodactyls who have come to you, and the chick they sent as emissary, also for forgiveness, because you seem to be able to forgive anyone or anything. I still don't know what they did, because you don't seem to either, but I am guessing they are serial killers, too, if I know my Nora. Some kind of extraterrestrial Nazis."

As though the terrestrial ones weren't enough, Nora thought. She remembered Heidegger, so popular now in ontical and ontological studies, joining the Nazi party, not out of conviction, but to further his career. She never could read him. But Nietzsche, a Russian professor out of some philological institute, maybe the Gorky, had told her that the mad syphilitic's (or was it cancer, as they now thought?) last words were "Death to anti-Semites." How he wept when the horse in the street was beaten! She somehow could not separate their critical stances from their lives. Look, just look at the ideologues, at Marx's children starving and Rousseau's abandoned. Fine flying on paper, but in reality, nasty, brutish, and short. Was Hobbes short, she wondered....

Michael shouted through her thoughts. "Nora, where are you? You're blocking me. Don't fight me, honey, I really do love you. Would I go to all this trouble, take all these risks, if I didn't? This is what they sing about, Nora."

Nora felt herself softening. She felt Michael's glow. This nut really thought he was in love with her.

"No, baby, I don't think, I know. But you *are* softening." Michael sounded like a teenage boy. "Now tell me what you know. What I get is that they are here to save the universe from some scheme Ouspensky has dreamed up to destroy it, and that it is going to happen soon. I am the only one besides you who knows this and I happen to be the only one smart enough to help. And I don't want to die. So, let me in—show me what trust is, because I really don't know."

Nora blocked him with a bhajan: *Om namah shivaya.*

"Nora, this is urgent. How long can you hold out against the army that is coming for you with broken glass and a geode?"

He was right, Nora realized. This maniac was her best hope.

"Nora, I heard that!" Michael pressed his point. "Tell me everything, Nora," he cajoled. His voice was mellifluous, honeyed, understanding. Nora saw how easily his victims could succumb to his persuasion: *Let me give you a ride, sweetheart....*

"Nora, please, I heard that, too. But you know better than anyone else that I am not a sociopath, that I am sick, a psychopath, a victim of horrible childhood abuse, and I can't stop, I would if I knew how, but I need to abreact and you could do that for me. You know that. You know I want to change and am willing to die re-experiencing my childhood and the thousands of murders I have committed. I just want a letter from you once in a while in whatever facility they put me in, if they don't kill me. But somehow, I don't think you will let them kill me, if you can do anything to stop it. I want to be forgiven by you."

Nora knew he was telling the truth.

"What do you always say?" Michael sounded a bit desperate. "You haven't changed your mind?"

No, Nora thought, *not on that.*

"Well, say it!"

Nora's fought diarrhea as she thought of the girls slowly tortured, skinned alive, and stuffed into the silken skins Michael had designed for them as he came in repeated ecstasy.

"Nora, not now. In the name of Christ, Nora, say it!"

Nora exhaled. She started haltingly, "It is either forgiveness of all sins ..."

"Please, Nora, say it. It's the only thing I live for."

Nora shook herself. It was true, after all, and she would say it. She continued loudly, so that Michael could feel her certainty.

"It is forgiveness of all sins, *all* sins, or it is all bullshit. But it is not bullshit."

Nora felt Michael's gratitude. For a moment the kind and dull-witted photographer entered mad Michael's mind. His screams were the loudest Nora had ever heard.

"My God, that's enough to make me stop!"

Nora shook her head. "You are lying, Michael. He'll think it was a nightmare. You haven't scratched the surface."

"Yes, I'm lying. But I will fully abreact one day and you will help me. But now I need to help you. Tell me about the birds and Ouspensky. Does he know about them?"

"He can probably hear." Nora thought hard. Who was listening? Who hadn't she called out in the last few days in this bold attempt at transparency, challenging, daring the perps to kill her, making herself bigger and badder than she was. But the bluff might work. They might think she had allies. And it might have bought time.

Even the Birds, the great secret that must be kept from these monsters—would it be so bad if they thought she had powerful alien friends? Did they need to know the great pterodactyls were blind and broken in spirit, traveling an interstellar *hadj* to atone for ancient, unpardonable guilt?

"Nora ..."

She ignored the voice inside her head. She could stay alive for a few more days, maybe get to China or Syria. Maybe her friends could help. She still had some, like Audrey. And Andrew, the CIA chief; he liked her, had asked her to go ice skating once—why hadn't she gone? Fear of falling. He could be trusted, she knew that. But most were terrified of her now. She was a marked woman. Marked for assassination, marked for the private, personal hell Deal and Ouspensky were designing for her even at this moment. Dear loving Genya ...

"Dammit," Michael interrupted," I am smarter and stronger than your disgusting choice of love addiction. And a better fuck, given half a chance. Here's what I know; we can think freely in your little mental cave here. You do trust me for some reason."

Unwillingly, Nora mentally nodded.

Michael was exuberant. "Listen: you are letting me in; you are letting me help you? I've never done this before. Nora, this is better than a hard-on."

"Michael ..."

"Okay—the Birds are blind and have come to you for help regaining their sight. They have warned you that Ouspensky has armed four particle accelerators to recreate the Big Bang in reverse, to blow the cosmos out of existence just for the hell of it. Have I gotten it?"

Nora mentally nodded again.

"Now I know all this and can help you. Because," his voice swelled with pride, "I really am smarter than Ouspensky."

Nora was nervous. "Michael, can they hear?"

"Nope. You, see, my mind is powerful enough to block them. And see straight into you. You truly believe I am sick and not bad?" Michael was pleased with himself. "Impressed? Tell me I'm smarter than Ouspensky."

Nora mentally shook her head. "It will turn you on."

"True," Michael agreed. "Just the thought of it—wait, I have to jack off again. God, this is fun!"

Nora felt the seismic jolt of Michael's ejaculation. It was hot.

"I heard that!" Michael said. "Maybe we could do this together, me jerking off like a normal guy? Can I come in?"

"No, Michael. You are not a normal guy."

"I am when I am with you. We could try. I'd just like to have sex with a live woman once in my life and then asphyxiate her, instead of the other way around."

"*MICHAEL!*" Nora commanded.

"Okay, I'm not going anywhere." Michael sighed. "Okay, I'm in control now. Your blind birds need a retinal pigment to restore their sight. They can then help us stop Ouspensky—I said us, Nora, because I really am your friend. The Birds need a certain neon bluish-greenish retinal pigment, but no such pigment exists on Earth."

"Let me guess," Nora ventured.

"Yes, my dear—you do admire me a little, don't you? I've just invented it. I am a pretty brilliant photographer and do know something about light and color. I can run a batch up from my cave in a couple of weeks. Your ugly ducklings from Cygnus will see and be our army to save the planet. That will be some penance for me, right, saving the world? And do you realize I read the Birds' minds just now through yours? Can Ouspensky do that?"

Nora suddenly felt terror and the feeling was neither hers nor Michael's. Her insides turned to water. "Michael, do you have a live girl with you now?"

There was a pregnant pause in Nora's consciousness.

"Dear God, she's pregnant!" Nora exclaimed in horror.

"Variety is the spice of life," Michael answered coldly. "Don't mess with my kill, bitch."

"Fuck you!!!" Nora screamed.

"They heard that," Michael cautioned.

"This conversation is over!"

"You can't block me like the others."

"No? Try me." Nora concentrated, powered by terror and rage.

Nora sensed a vacuum, like a will receding. "Okay, I let her go," Michael said almost humbly.

"I thought you were manacled."

"I do keep the keys, darling. I tell you things to make you feel secure."

"I do not feel secure."

"The kill is gone, run screaming into the night. She's going to lead the moron detectives here. I will have to make tracks. But I have proven to you what your friendship is worth to me, right? Nora, where are you? You have blocked me! I'm serious; I let her and the fetus go."

"Really?"

"You can hear me and I can't hear you unless you let me? Nora, you are not so dumb yourself."

What was it with the men in her life? Nora wondered. "Never said I was, Michael. I have to make the calls to turn you in."

"Damn, you really can block me out. Must be some female thing. Bye for now. I'll be back soon."

***

Nora inhaled deeply as Michael left her mind. The clangs had stopped. The clangs were exactly the kind of Skinnerian torture Deal would come up with. Her wonderful first psychiatrist and psychoanalyst, Deal: ignorant and grandiose, ambitious as Lucifer, and brutally sexist. Over the ten-year course of their therapy, he PET-scanned and became interested in Nora's unique brain, with its thin corpus callosum, often thinner in females, but in hers almost absent, allowing extraordinary interconnectivity between her left and right hemispheres. And a peculiar, arrhythmic action of the sodium-potassium pump. This, Nora knew, was probably as far as the moron had gotten. But he knew how to cut and tear, and cut and tear Nora's brain Deal was determined to do.

As unsavory as Deal was, and as horrible her treatment if she fell into his hands, he was essentially a flunky who needed big men to order him around. No, it was

The Howard and Ussasis and Prince Ouspensky, Nora's Satanist and transvestite lover, who called the shots. And these had small interest in Deal's scientific ambitions or Deal's Mexican pain lab. They just wanted the children in his research trials because they liked buggering them. And watching them suffer as Deal systematically lowered the levels of analgesics he administered before torturing them, all for fun and a more effective headache pill.

But although they were vastly wealthier than him, even The Howard and Ussasis bowed before Prince Eugene Ouspensky. A scion of Naryshkin blood and a lineal descendent of Peter the Great, the model for Dr. Frankenfurter in *The Rocky Horror Show*, Ouspensky's royalty and genius and magnetism drew all the powerbrokers, moneymen, and one-percenters to him. Rich Arabs and movie stars and heads of state flocked to his parties and tittered at a moment of recognition from him.

Nora had easily succumbed to his blandishments; she remembered his erotic imagination and the tidal wave of their sex—and noticed her cunt twitched madly as she did, even knowing what she knew about him. Ouspensky, *Genya* to his intimates, was a consummately skilled lover, making other men seem like apes, frogs depositing their sperm on rocks.

Genya could also mimic human emotions masterfully. When he wasn't grunting over a three-year-old girl; Nora forced herself to that memory, obscured by her lust. Ouspensky could make you forget about that. And he was certainly the most intelligent man on the planet, a twisted polymath who really knew how to throw a party.

Nora surveyed the wreckage of the apartment again. There wasn't much time left. She recapped: So, The Howard wanted her dead but wouldn't off her because Ouspensky had other plans, and neither would Ussasis. They wanted Nora's brain, Nora's peculiar brain, and Deal would keep her alive in his Mexican torture chamber for tots in whatever new cryogenic device Ouspensky had invented for this purpose, hacking up her spine, amygdala, cerebellum, and cerebrum, dissecting them, then replacing them with Ouspensky's AI devices and then freezing and thawing the whole mess again until … until what?

"Okay, Deal," she said aloud. "What is organic?" Nora imagined Deal frantically phoning the poor graduate student who answered these questions for him. Was Deal even a doctor? It didn't really matter. He knew enough to follow instructions, and Ouspensky would make those crystal clear.

It had gotten complex lately, Nora acknowledged to herself. And many had been called out in Nora's desperate last stand. Most recently, of course, she had discovered and publicized the DNA trail that confirmed who killed Jack Kennedy. This, it seemed to Nora, was a no-brainer for any detective; she had it figured out before she even got her license. Who wouldn't get pissed off if her man was publicly doing Marilyn Monroe?

And she had outed The Howard as a baby bugger. Had to, really—his appetite was increasing. But he was on Ouspensky's leash, at least for the time being. And the participants in dear Genya's black masses, those revelers in human sacrifice, torture, and rape, Nora had outed them, and their best efforts at cover-up had failed. Yes, Nora had pissed off a lot of people.

And now there were the Birds, the huge flying penitents, who had come to Nora, of all the people on the planet, for help.

Which led to the questions again: Who was sending these clangs and hoodoo messages? Who was receiving hers? Andrew and the CIA, to toughen her, school her? Not everyone who puts you in shit is your enemy, she reflected; not everyone who pulls you out is your friend. Who was monitoring, jamming them? Who wanted her insane or dead? At Brookhaven, Deal even now was trying to interpret the PET scans of her thoughts. *Good luck with that, big boy,* she thought ruefully.

There was a time when the double bind, Deal's primitive form of torture, *you're good, you're bad*, used to work. The strong negative and hateful messages interleaved with love, the classic torturer's mindfuck, once might have stopped her. The technique was used, after all, because it was so effective. But not now: she had broken through. Nora had, after all, been doublebinded since birth by her mother … not the time to think about Mama now. Mama just wanted her dead.

Who were her friends? There was a hit on her, a lot of money by now and likely increasing every day, and friends could turn on a dime, she knew that. And while the main perps wanted her alive, there were enough amateurs out there to just kill her outright. And it wouldn't be a clean bullet to the head. Nora didn't fear poison, could always sense clean food, but a dirty shiv or boxcutter across the neck was unpleasant.

Nora blinked, and the image of an ISIS beheading, slow and gory, crossed the room.

They would probably send an old lady or a kid. Or someone who looked like her godchild and niece Tara, not huge and fat as she became, but as she once was, a radiant blonde and blue-eyed child. Of course, she would hesitate seeing the one being she had loved enough to die for. And she'd be dead.

The big hit money was actually irrelevant; they could easily find someone to do it for the price of a burger. They had armies of weak and impoverished people at their beck and call. Nora had never killed anyone, and they knew that. Would she be able to kill to save her life? Nora truly didn't know, but she wanted to live, even under these circumstances.

The gruesome images and obscene commands were now visible and audible again. A disgusting scatological mass hovered over her, eating the planet city by city, region by region, leaving nothing but shit in its wake. Ouspensky liked to eat the contents of diapers, she recalled; this looked like his work.

"You are passing the test with flying colors," the announcer voice said again. *Good cop, bad cop,* thought Nora. The REM sleep kept her from succumbing, but even with it, she didn't know how long she could hold out. She had to get out of the house.

And go where? China, Tibet, Syria …

She was overthinking this. She turned on YouTube and blasted Kurtis Blow: *And you borrowed money from the mob / them's the breaks, them's the breaks / and yesterday, you lost your job.*

Time for a meeting.

Nora picked up her phone; it still worked. She dialed into the Sex and Love Addicts Anonymous phone bridge. It was the partnership meeting, and the qualifier, Ted B., was acknowledging that he did not respect his sex-addict liaison partners. There was something familiar about the voice, not familiar from the rooms, but odd, out of place.

Ted B. was telling his listeners that he was omitting graphic acting-out details that might trigger someone. He shared that dealing with the will of another human being was too much for him and that he had trouble turning his own over to a higher power. This egocentrism had blocked him until recently from partnership and true love....

It was Michael. Nora hung up the phone.

I'm a Bundy girl. I love serial killers, she reflected. *No wonder I'm a cop, I fucking love perps. Or love fucking them. Whatever.* She lay down on the couch. The transmitter beeped and activated again.

FLASHBACK: Truman Capote's black-and-white party, which we see is a Black Mass presided over by Genya Ouspensky. Satanic priests administering cannibalistic hosts. A young Nora is there in white tux and tails, doting on the head warlock as the wealthy and fashionable crowd looks at images of the dead Kansas family from *In Cold Blood* and at the killers in their cells, sweating, hoping for a phone call from their friend Truman who is lobbying for their execution so that he can finish his book. The crucifix on the wall, *pace* Lenny Bruce, is a Kansas electric chair, primitive, wooden, with the ultimate in S&M bondage straps....

Nora dances for the assembled crowd, a witty tap. She sees Ouspensky take a Shirley Temple look-alike upon his knees. She finishes her dance with the same angry gesture Columbia makes during the Time Warp segment of *Rocky Horror*, disgusted with Ouspensky, and, God forgive her, jealous....

Nora sat bolt upright. "Okay, okay," she said aloud. "It is either forgiveness of all sins, *all sins,* or it is all bullshit, my own sins and bullshit included."

And the flashback faded, and there was Ouspensky, tall, black-maned and blue-eyed, standing before her, his confident yet vulnerable smile no flashback, but sensuously and immediately real. Nora's hormones went off the charts. There was no point in pretending; Ouspensky knew quite well the effect he had on Nora.

He sat down on the couch next to her, placing a long muscular leg between Nora's thighs. "Hello, *solnishko,*" he said in his flawless English and muscovite Russian.

"You make me sick," Nora told him honestly.

Ouspensky laughed and Nora heard the *Ode to Joy* ring out. He took her in his arms. "I make you well. You know I can. You know you want me to. But this is inelegant." Ouspensky turned Nora's face toward him, his eyes knowing, loving, daring, his thigh touching her thighs, his spine the exact curvature of hers. "Let's catch up, dear."

"Just because I want to doesn't mean I have to." Kiss.

"Lovely 12-step pablum." Longer kiss.

"The plastic surgeon does a good job, Genya. You look youthful, in a Frankensteinish way."

Ouspensky smiled and kissed her again, and for Nora

the kisses *surpass bodily geography finding light finding the other finding laughing losing self losing control this is the only true hallelujah ...*

MICHAEL (TO THE READER) Okay, enough of that shit. I would have killed him by now except that there are three hundred cops paid off by Ouspensky surrounding Nora's apartment. Not that I wouldn't have been successful despite that, but I realized that the sight of Nora moaning and climaxing, or worse, lying there completely satisfied, would be too much for me; I really would kill her and fuck her then and there after I dispatched her great genius like a fly. So, I used, God help me, good judgment. Restraint. Forbearance.

She's passed out. He's lifting her up in his arms. He's taking her somewhere. I'll follow.

***

As Ouspensky carried Nora out the front door, Michael looked up and saw the Birds, a dozen of them, kettling around the roof of Nora's building. He almost forgot about Nora. They were like huge leathery eagles or swans or bats, beautiful in a magnificent saurian way. They were singing, a plaintive, unearthly song, sounding like harmonious metallic gulls. Michael thought he heard strains of Bach. A throng had gathered to gawk at them, held back by the police.

So, this is wonder, Michael thought. *Maybe there is a God.*

He snapped to. *Ouspensky knows about the Birds now for sure*, Michael realized. *Everybody does.*

Michael slipped past the army of plainclothes detectives and uniforms congregating on West 72nd Street. An ambulance wailed up to Nora's building, and Ouspensky, dressed as a paramedic, helped to carry an unconscious Nora out on a stretcher. Michael knew they were taking her to Deal's lab.

The 'lance forced its way through traffic on Central Park West with a convoy of police cars following. Michael followed in a stolen police car, blending in. The fleet of crooked and duped cops and their Satanic boss crossed the 65th Street thoroughfare through the park and turned onto Second Avenue, forcing cars to roll onto the pavement as they headed—where? Toward the bridge to Queens? The airport and on to Mexico, Michael surmised.

No, Michael was wrong: the 'lance turned onto the upper roadway of the Koch Bridge, and then picked up the Long Island Expressway out to Woodhaven Boulevard. There, the cop cars dispersed, with only a few still following the 'lance as it headed east. With a series of turns that looked like Ouspensky was shaking tails, the 'lance stopped before a squat brick structure in Middle Village with coke and ash covering a brick chimney. A crematorium.

Michael parked the cop car in the crematorium parking lot and waited.

Ouspensky emerged from the 'lance and entered the building. Michael took his chance. There were other two men in the 'lance, a driver and another EMT. He knocked both out with his fists.

And there was Nora, Nora in four-point restraint,

her unconscious form beautiful even with her tongue hanging out. Michael realized he had never been this close to her before, never seen her body or face in such detail, that he could touch her if he wanted to, that he could …

Ouspensky's return with a stretcher interrupted Michael's lust. He looked at the unconscious bodies of his henchmen, and then at Michael.

"What the fuck is this?" Ouspensky snarled at Michael. "Who the fuck are you?"

I could kill him now, Michael reflected. *It would be fun.* Michael imagined his rival's corpse with barely suppressed glee. *Forbearance,* he thought. *Let's see what this pimp is up to.*

"Distefano, Boss. Boss, they were calling someone. It sounded funny. I figured I had better put them on ice till I told you," Michael explained in his best Brooklyn accent.

"Kill them," Ouspensky ordered. Michael willingly complied.

"Now put her on the stretcher."

Michael lifted Nora's unconscious form and was filled with a feeling that he could not identify. Tenderness, he guessed. *This is holding a real live girl?* he thought. *This is not just hot, this is nice, like oatmeal, or something.*

"Hurry up, asshole." Michael interrupted his reverie to take a good look at his rival. Tall, muscular, brutal. *But old*, Michael reflected. *I can take him in my sleep.*

Ouspensky and Michael carried Nora into the entrance of the crematorium to a large elevator that was as out of place in the brick structure as a living body in a bier. A huge titanium door with an array of hi-tech sensors over the call buttons: facial recognition software, eye scans, hand scan, an argon-laser motion tracker, digital recorders, and a strange device, laser-powered by an element Michael had never seen before.

With a brusque "Fuck off!" Ouspensky shut down the sensor array. The elevator opened and Michael wheeled Nora in.

The elevator had only down buttons, 300 of them. Strobe lights washed the interior. Michael looked at the round head of Ouspensky, imagining it squashed like a pumpkin in his hands.

Nora suddenly came to consciousness, delirious.

"Darling Nora," Ouspensky trilled. "You like paramedics, darling."

The delirious Nora looked at Ouspensky without recognition. "Yes," she muttered, "Brave. They go into all kinds of scary places unarmed." She tried to sit up and couldn't because of the restraints. Confused, she passed out again.

Ouspensky took a large serrated knife out of his pocket and ran it across her sleeping neck. "Not always unarmed, *querida*," he told her unconscious form.

The elevator stopped at a large mezzanine. Below them, Michael saw a corridor of what looked like hotel rooms, numbered but with wide doors open. Inside, he saw men and women dressed in period costumes, Restoration, antebellum south, old Russe. There was a lot of copulation going on, and much more besides. Michael saw one man in a farmer's straw hat eagerly fucking a pig. The players saw Ouspensky and cheered, not stopping their activities.

"Remember, the more you pay, the more you play," Ouspensky reminded his audience. A hologram of a vending machine appeared and hovered beneath the mezzanine ceiling. Several players scrambled to the corners of their rooms, where the real vending machines stood.

Ouspensky smiled contemptuously. The elevator doors shut silently. Michael decided he would kill the old fart now and moved closer to his prey. But the elevator stopped again.

This was -220, according to the neon-blue light on the panel. The doors opened and Michael saw a war room with maps of Russia and the United States lit up by radar tracking systems. Michael saw the Secretary of State and The Howard among the men huddled around the huge conference room table in the center of the room. Hillary Clinton lay on the table wriggling, bound and gagged.

"If we hit them now," The Howard began. The Secretary of State interrupted with vigorous grunting noises that sounded like *no*. He sounded like a man without a tongue. Which he was, Michael determined.

Ouspensky addressed the generals and politicians. "You are engaged in nuclear war games, with actual warheads. Your bombers are about to blow up the Eastern seaboard of the United States, stopping just short of detonation. But who knows? One lucky winner may go all the way!" The vending machine hologram appeared and hung in the air. The Howard ran to the real thing.

Michael weighed his options. Kill the fart now? God, he wanted to. But Nora would be disappointed if he didn't save the Birds, prevent nuclear war, and disarm Ouspensky's particle accelerators. So, he should wait.

Ouspensky steered Nora into a small hospital room at -290 with another vending machine in the corner. Ouspensky removed her pants and underwear, and partially lifted the sheet covering her, exposing her unshaven cunt. He left her there alone on the stretcher.

Men dressed like Tolkien's Nazgûl, dark, hooded beings, slowly entered the room one by one. Michael could see hatchets and knives like scimitars beneath their robes. They gathered in a circle around Nora, looking at her labia, drooling.

Michael was alarmed. *They will tear her to pieces,* he thought, forgetting for a moment his own cock's reaction to Nora's pink and wet folds.

The observation lasted only minutes. Fluorescent lights flooded the room. "Time's up!" a game-show-host voice announced. The Nazgûl scrambled for their wallets and eagerly inserted credit cards and hundred-dollar bills into the vending machine.

"Come back tomorrow," the game-show host commanded. Ouspensky wheeled Nora out of the room and the Nazgûl dispersed.

Down again, -300, the last button in the elevator array.

Bottom floor, Michael wondered? No. A flight of Escher-like stairs with a neon sign above them: Hades. Deal's New York lab. *Nine levels, of course.*

Following Ouspensky, Michael entered a large laboratory with a huge suspended tank filled with a bluish-white fluid, cryogenic equipment, a PET scan, surgical tables. And again, a laser device powered by the same element as in the elevator.

He watched as Deal and Ouspensky immersed Nora into the tank and activated the laser.

What the hell is that? Michael scanned the rare gases in his mind, then the semiconductors, and then the entire periodic table. *No, no, no. What the fuck is …*

They have a fucking new element, Michael realized. *Maybe this Ouspensky clown is smarter than I thought.*

As Deal and Ouspensky watched the monitors, Michael despaired. *These aren't teenagers from Jersey,* he thought. He caught himself. *Ouspensky may be smart,* he grudgingly acknowledged. *And he has an edge because he doesn't give a shit about her. But I do, and that gives* me *an edge, one Ouspensky can't dream of.*

Michael paused as a new sensation came over him, one like the wonder he felt upon seeing the Birds. *I do love her,* he realized. *And I am going to get her the hell out of here.*

"You," Ouspensky commanded Michael. "Get the fuck out of here."

Kill them now. Kill them now. Get her out of here.

A gang of men who looked like Orcs from a Tolkien book suddenly appeared and surrounded him.

"Throw him into the furnace," Ouspensky ordered.

Kill him now. No, wait. "I helped you, Boss; I can help you again."

"Okay, if you can get out of the furnace, you can live." Ouspensky laughed heartily. "Boys, put him in -211 and let the sexual sadists know we're frying today. Burn him a little first for the hologram and let's hear some real screaming."

"Boss …" *Stall. An opportunity may arise. Stall.*

Ouspensky appraised Michael. "Not bad looking. Tell Mammon to do a ladies' special and charge double."

Stall. "I love you, boss. Let me help you."

"Shut up. Get him out of here."

I have to leave her here, case the joint, look for a way out. Goodbye for now, darling, I'll be back.

***

As the orcs led Michael out of Hades, Nora came to in the tank, a cheap snorkel attached to her mouth and nose. Oxygen tanks and electronic monitors surrounded her, and she was chained and manacled like Houdini.

Where am I?

How do I get out of here?

Can I get out of here?

Not my body. My mind. Go away now, Nora.

Trance. Speak, memory.

FLASHBACK: Ouspensky's chalet at the foot of Mont Blanc in Switzerland. A vast underground chamber. Nora is seventeen. She is a breeder; Ouspensky's cult has been inseminating her and harvesting her fertilized eggs. Around her on the walls in a blood-red organic matrix are fetuses being fed through tubes. And on the floor in cages, more children, two, three years old. Hers.

A party is going on. She is sitting on a throne next to Ouspensky, dressed as a Satanic queen. She is in chains. Drunken revelers, paid guests, faces painted black and white, reel all around. Ouspensky offers her the purest grade heroin; Nora smiles and pretends to snort it, sneezing and coughing and laughing uproariously to expel the substance from her nostrils. She acts high, leaning into Ouspensky's face and slurring *I love yous* to him, dripping saliva on his cloak. Out of the corner of her terrified eyes, she is watching the cages.

In the corner of the cavern is an electrical outlet with boxes attached by gray cords. A video camera rotates, scanning the room; Ouspensky is filming the festivities for sale as hard-core S&M porn.

Nora screams, "I want to dance, I want to dance," and Ouspensky, amused, removes her manacles and cuffs. She stands and deliberately falls at the foot of the throne. She lifts herself up, pretends to vomit, stumbles over to the outlet. *Think. Video equipment. Can you make a bomb out of recording equipment? Vodka. Molotov cocktail. Gasoline. Where is gasoline? Ouspensky's car? Get him to take me to his car.*

Vodka, gasoline, electrical wires, electric fire. Get them out in the chaos. Think.

Nora looks around the room. The sight is horror, but it is the sound, the sound, the piercing constant cries of the children that is unbearable. Crying, screaming, calling for *Mama*. Nora falls, overwhelmed.

Think.

She tries to raise herself but can't. The babies are screaming; high-pitched, pure screams of terror. She falls again.

THINK, DON'T FEEL.

She presses her cheek to the cool stone floor. "I can't, I can't bear," she whispers. "It is too much, oh god oh god oh god shut my ears. . . ."

I have to do something. I have to do something. Vodka. Wires. Electrical fire.

I can't.

You can. You can. You can. God, god damn you, do something. Help me.

She vomits. She lies in the pool of puke,

Please, bozinka, *my child's* Bog, *where are you?* Pomogi.

Damn you, pomogi*!*

Bozinka. *God. HEY, YOU!*

You are silent. Is this your will? IS THIS YOUR FUCKING WILL?

Think. Don't feel.

Anger. Feel anger. Anger is strong.

RAGE. STRONGER.

OKAY: IF YOU MOTHERFUCKER GOD WON'T HELP ME, THEN SATAN, SATAN: SATAN, TAKE ME. TAKE ME, GIVE ME STRENGTH. YOU FUCKING GOD, IS THIS THY WILL? FUCK THAT. SATAN, HELP ME, SATAN. MAKE ME STRONG.

SPLIT.

AH.

SPLIT NOW.

NORA IS GONE.

THE PREDATOR IS BORN.

AND I MUST.

AND I WILL.

THANK YOU, DEAR SATAN, GREAT DIVIDER! YOU RULE! COMMAND ME! WHAT IS YOUR WILL?

DON'T LOOK AT THEM. THEY DO NOT EXIST. THEY ARE NOT YOUR CHILDREN. THEY ARE RATS IN CAGES SQUEALING. DON'T THINK ABOUT THEM. THINK.

COCAINE; IT WILL KILL THE PAIN, MAKE YOU

ALERT. HAVE A CIGARETTE; NICOTINE IS GOOD FOR CONCENTRATION.

Nora rises and smiles. She waltzes back to Ouspensky and gives him a blowjob. It is a good one.

GENYA *DOROGOI, PODAI MNE KOKAINY. SPASIBO, MOI TSAR. A PAPIROSA. SPASIBO MILY MOI.*

IT'S A FUCKING PARTY. HAVE A BALL.

Genya feeds Nora cigarettes, cocaine and vodka. The revelers laugh at her addictiveness.

NOW THIS IS GOOD. I FEEL FINE. STRONG. I CAN DO ANYTHING. GENYA, YOU WANT TO PUT YOUR CIGARETTE OUT ON MY CUNT, DEAR ONE? BEFORE THAT, LET ME PUT A LITTLE *KOKAINA* ON YOUR HUGE AND MAGNIFICENT COCK....

One by one the revelers pass out on the floor of the cavern.

More cocaine, another blowjob. Nora's teeth viciously and intentionally scrape Ouspensky's dick. He yelps, slaps her. He starts to leave the hall.

WHERE ARE YOU GOING, MY LORD?

"I'm going to sleep, you sloppy cow. I've had enough of you for a year."

I'M SLEEPY, TOO. CAN I COME WITH YOU, HEE HEE? DON'T LEAVE ME HERE ALL ALONE.

"Leave me alone."

Ouspensky tells a flunky to be sure and collect all the money from the participants and leaves the room.

STAND. STRETCH. I FEEL GOOD. ROPE AROUND MY FEET. STOLY BOTTLE. DRINK. BREAK. GLASS. BROKEN GLASS. THAT WILL WORK. GOOD.

I WANT TO DANCE. WHY ARE YOU ALL ASLEEP?

I WANT TO DANCE. ONE TWO THREE. GLASS. BROKEN GLASS. THROAT. CUT THROAT. ONE THROAT, TWO THROATS, THREESIES, FOURSIES; FLUNKEY THROAT HAS A GRAM OF COCAINE IN HIS POCKET THANK YOU AND ONE TWO THREE AND WE ARE DONE. ALL THROATS CUTSY-WHATSIE.

THE RATS.

CAN BEND THE CAGE BARS. SURE I CAN. STEE-RONG!

LEAVE THE FETUS RATS. CAN'T TAKE THE FETUS RATS. TWELVE CAGE RATS TO TAKE AWAY. TWO AT A TIME. TWO INTO TWELVE IS SIX. FIRE ESCAPE. HIGH. CLIMB, KOKAINA!

UP UP AND AWAY. STOLY FOR MY TRIP. TWOSIES, CHICKEN FAT. FOURSIES, CHICKEN FAT.

Snowy. Cold. Will die here, lost cold road. Lost. I die here, too.

DON'T FEEL. I AM THINKING.

ROAR! THERE YOU GO! MOTORCYCLE, BMW. RICH. TALK TO HIM, NORA. CRY.

SICK RATS. CRY MORE.

FOURSIES RATS IN THE HOSPITAL.

GET MORE RATS. RATS IN THE HOSPITAL, RATS IN THE HOSPITAL, FUNNY! WE ARE HAVING FUN!

When Nora returns to the chamber for the rest of her children, Ouspensky is there. She is beaten and chained. Two of her remaining children are used for sex and sacrificed on a black mass altar before her eyes.

I am the dead girl. I am dead. The dead do not feel, the dead do not hear. I am the dead girl, I don't hear them crying, I I I I.

I am the deaf girl, I am the blind girl, I I I I I.

Inviting new revelers, Ouspensky organizes a line of men to sodomize Nora.

LIKE WE NEED COCAINE TO FEEL GOOD? I'M HIGH ON LIFE. BRING IT ON, BOYS!

There are six remaining children, apart from the fetuses. Their plight does not seem to affect Nora; she is impassive and does not seem to be suffering.

Ouspensky understands that Nora is not broken yet. Something has to be done. He looks at Nora with new malice. Good cop, bad cop. He decides to make love to her as if he truly loved her. Ouspensky gently carries her to his bed. He nurses her, drugs her with roofies. He reads the *Lettres de la Jeune Portugaise* to her. He courts her, writes poetry to her, role-plays as Pushkin and adores her small feet. The battered Nora finally succumbs to him and forgets about her children for days and weeks. *He loves me....*

In an unguarded moment, Ouspensky whispers Nora's true identity to her: Nora is Larissa Ekaterina Anastasia Nikolayevna Romanova, heir to the throne of Russia. After a brief nuclear war which will destroy the United States and Israel, she is to rule the Russian empire, the Persian Gulf, India, and China with Ouspensky as her consort and de facto Tsar. Nora knows this is true. She realizes that she speaks flawless Russian and French, has an exhaustive knowledge of history and geopolitics, plays chess at the grandmaster level, and is an expert markswoman. She is a princess of the blood royal, to be Tsarina after Putin and rival nations are disposed with. She comes to herself and hates Ouspensky.

Larissa artfully dodges sex with Ouspensky by role playing Anna and Vronsky, Lara and Zhivago, and he enjoys this. During their verbal intercourse, she hides her disgust and thinks of the cavern. She thinks of her children and their cries. She knows who she is now. She bides her time.

She distracts Ouspensky. She praises his derivative poetry. She writes poetry to him in French and Russian. She flatters him and draws him out to learn his plans; a Scheherazade now, she keeps him from the cavern and its barbaric rituals and her children.

Nora cooks for Ouspensky. He likes almonds, apricots. She saves the pits and some of the nuts.

Trusted by Ouspensky now, she sneaks away to the chamber in the mornings to sit near her children and sing to them, tell them stories. She has prepared cyanide from the almonds and apricots and steels herself to feed the pale blue powder to them. They are so small and weak, it will not take much. But she cannot bring herself to administer the poison.

She is caught. The alters Nora, Larissa, Predator make a last stand. They rush to the center of the chamber and shout and sing at the top of their lungs. Nora yells "Fire!" and "Rape!" and calls for the police. Larissa calls upon Jesus, Shiva, Chango, and Satan to save her children. The Predator overpowers ten of Ouspensky's thugs, but finally, is captured, chained.

The rituals begin again. Nora is forced to watch.

Ouspensky wants Nora to perform the final sacrifice, kill the last remaining child. Defeated, Larissa quietly but firmly says *no.* The Predator and Dead Girl offer help, but she refuses.

"Thank you, Predator, but your services are no longer needed," Nora and Larissa reply. "Dear Dead Girl, thank you, too; rest in peace, I will join you soon."

Larissa is put kneeling and naked into a chair and blindfolded. Ouspensky holds a revolver to her temple. Larissa prays the *Oche Nash* aloud to teach it to Nora, says *Ta budet volya tvoia*, and falls silent.

GET SOME KOKAINA AND WE'LL TURN THE GUN ON HIM AND …

Thank you, dear Predator, but it's over.

Nora prepares to die as the Baron Albert Bensinck, the owner of the BMW motorcycle who saved some of Nora's children, enters the chamber with two Swiss police, having suspected foul play there. He recognizes Nora and confronts Ouspensky. Ouspensky's thugs kill the Swiss police and the Baron, realizing he must get help, escapes with his life, reluctantly abandoning Nora to her fate.

Ouspensky and Deal partially lobotomize Nora. Coming out of a coma in a Swiss hospital, she struggles, fights Deal, punches a cult nun. They lobotomize her again. She has no memory of the past months. Ouspensky enrolls her in a Swiss finishing school, where she gets good grades and wins the school's drama award . . .

***

Nora came out of the flashback and realized where she was. Deal's lab. Tired. Weak. Cryogenic equipment around the tank. They would soon freeze her, cut her brain, thaw, and cut again. This would go on till she was dead. That might not be for years.

Even now, I don't have the will to die, Nora thought. *Lord of Israel, do this for me. They will repeat this for many years and I will suffer. Help me to will myself to die.*

Nothing.

I don't hear you. Life and death are in your hands? Well, let's see about that. A gedanken *experiment: Can I will myself to die? Probably, outside of your reality. And I do believe I am now quite definitely outside your reality. Does not Satan have his bailiwick? I am in Hell. I call upon Satan then. Satan, lord of the flies, Beelzebub, Lucifer, angel of darkness, help me.*

I take my will back. I am alone. I am singing "My Way." I separate myself from you, God of Abraham and Mohammed, sky God, God of sheep, God of fools.

There you go; my life force is ebbing. I am thinking myself to death. Here is the exercise of my will, Jehovah. I choose to die. You give me that choice, you are a God of choice, once were my God of choice. You killed my children. God of love? Not so much, I think. I think; therefore, I don't exist. I die.

"The monitors are dropping. She's flatlining," Deal cried.

"You fucked this up," Ouspensky barked.

"It's not my fault," Deal squealed.

"Get her the fuck out of there, you asshole!"

Deal and Ouspensky removed Nora from the tank.

Ouspensky slapped Deal. "She's remembering!"

"No, she can't!" Deal whined.

"Yes, the bitch is remembering. Look at her face. She's fucking Larissa again."

"I cut it out…" Deal began.

"Well, cut it out again."

They set Nora, barely alive, in a chair. Deal poised a long, thin needle at her right eye. Nora emitted a long, high-pitched scream of terror and passed out.

***

Having killed his orc guard, Michael explored floor -211. He found a room with monitors, flat screens, couches. *The voyeur room*, he concluded. He flipped on the TV.

YOUSUCK, the black and red logo blared. A Nazi flag waved proudly beneath it.

Michael flipped the channels. The lab. Deal pointing a foot-long needle at Nora's eye. Michael was fascinated. *Maybe I could do that to one of my dolls,* he mused, belatedly realizing that he should be having protective feelings to mobilize him to Nora's rescue.

This is a lobotomy, he concluded. They fuck with her that way, fuck with her memory. How often have they done this?

Michael watched as Deal took out a tray of scalpels.

"If the needle doesn't work," Deal was saying, "I'll do a frontal. I saw one of my students do it once."

Ouspensky slapped Deal again. "Alive, you quack. We still need her alive. Broken, but alive. The fucking little bitch needs to be broken. Fucking cunt scraped my dick with her teeth. I'm not letting her off so easy." Ouspensky considered his options. He turned to face the cowering psychiatrist. "You're an idiot, Deal. I'm putting Hawk on her."

Hatred lit Deal's face. "That bitch? She'll fuck everything up."

Ouspensky ignored him. "Paula, I need you," he spoke into an intercom.

A smooth female voice answered. "At your service, your royal highness. Multiples therapy on the prisoner?"

"Your best, Paula. See what she remembers."

Orcs carried the nearly lifeless Nora to a cozy room. Michael tracked their movements on the screen. *The -300 floor,* Michael noted. *The first circle. How do I get there?*

The orcs laid her on a couch with embroidered pillows and covered her with a down quilt. Nora slept. After a few minutes, liveried servants appeared and abruptly woke her. They carried the now-conscious Nora down the hall to Dr. Hawk's office.

Nora sat silently in the waiting room of Hawk's psychiatric office. A worn poster of Van Gogh's *Sunflowers* hung tackily on the wall. Hawk, a tall and muscular woman, confident and attractive, opened the office door and smiled at Nora. With a friendly nod, she invited her into her book-lined therapy room.

She looks like my Aunt Lena, Nora thought. *She was probably selected for that reason.* Nora stared at the psychiatrist's thin ankles and sharply edged calves. *A cyclist,* Nora surmised.

She can't make me talk to her, Nora tried to convince herself. *Or can she? In my state? Yes. Yes, she can.*

Dr. Hawk smiled. "If you like, you can take a moment before we begin. We can just sit together and breathe. You can use a breath after such an ordeal."

Yes, Nora agreed, she could.

"Would you like something? A cup of coffee, perhaps?"

Yes, Nora realized, she would very much like a hot cup of coffee.

Nora! Larissa commanded.

Hawk poured golden black-brown liquid from what smelled like a freshly brewed pot of … was that Sumatra? Yes, Nora's favorite. And white, white, white cream from a tiny blue ceramic saucer … into a blue and white Wedgwood cup.

Hawk handed the coffee to Nora.

Good cop, bad cop. It's working. Nora sipped, and it was heaven.

Dead girl no coffee no cream. Dead Girl.

Let me alone! Sorry, Dead Girl, I can handle this.

Nora, they are duping you, Larissa insisted. *The coffee is drugged.*

Feels really nice, Larissa. Hot, nice.

Nora, wake up! This pleasure will be extremely short-lived and the concomitants, ghastly. Please let me help you. The drugs have no effect on me.

Larissa, not now, please. Just let me have my hit.

Hawk smiled. "You are talking to your alters, aren't you? Nora … may I call you Nora? Please call me Paula; Dr. Hawk is so formal. And we are equals. This is a democracy, Nora. I know that Dr. Deal didn't believe that. And unlike Dr. Deal, I have boundaries. Tell me about your alters. Who am I talking to now?"

Nora? Nora.

"Really? It doesn't seem so. Who are the alters? What are their names? Oh, I am forgetting my manners. Would you like a macaroon? Here, sweetheart."

Don't eat it, Larissa said sharply. *There are memory drugs in it.*

Nora bit into the macaroon in Hawk's hand.

Nora, they are drugging you, Larissa repeated.

Larissa, go away.

Dr. Hawk smiled and topped off Nora's coffee. "Of course: Nora. There really is only Nora. But we all have facets, all respond differently to different situations. We are all of us chameleons. We all compartmentalize and dissociate to some degree. It's human and natural." Hawk handed Nora another macaroon, which Nora grabbed and ate greedily.

Hawk continued. "But in the case of post-traumatic stress disorder and DID, these rifts become harmful, maladaptive—I know you argued with Deal about PTSD and your dissociation; you correctly diagnosed yourself as a survivor, but he lacked the skill and insight to understand that." Hawk sighed. "Psychiatry has not served you well, my dear! Just between you and me, Deal is an unbearably stupid quack."

She is trying to bond with me by identifying a common enemy, Nora thought weakly as Hawk placed the plate of macaroons in Nora's lap.

"Let's get to work, dear, then I'll let you take a well-deserved nap. At the chalet, who saved the children?"

Proudly: PREDATOR

"I heard you say Larissa when we were bathing you in the healing tank. Who is Larissa?"

Nora, Larissa commanded. *You never said* Larissa. *You are fully drugged now. Let me handle her interrogation.*

Nora smiled. "I am Larissa Nikolayevna Romanova, *tsaritsa* of the blood royal, heir to the throne of the Russian Empire."

No more, Nora. Lord God, help. Macaroons. Macaroons. Macaroons, Nora. Think of Jewish holidays. Remember the

Temple. Remember the Maccabees. Remember the Warsaw Ghetto. Remember, like the Jews against all odds, your God.

"Shut up, Larissa," Nora said aloud. The sugar and coffee made her happy. *When was the last time she was happy? It would be good to talk, talk, talk to a woman she is kind, she will help she hates Deal too....*

Predator, Larissa pleaded, *please do something.*

NOT ANGRY. TIRED.

Larissa, I'm very tired. No more Predator. We'll talk a little and then Aunt Paula will let us take a nap. Maybe she'll tuck us in. Blanky so nice, so nice.

Nora's head wobbled a bit and dropped to her chest.

"Do you like birds, Nora?" Deal asked. "I love birds. Do you?"

Nora sat bolt upright. She heard the clangs again. NOT THE BIRDS.

Good girl! A psalm of David, a King of Israel, who slew Goliath: The Lord is my light and my salvation; of whom shall I be afraid? The Lord is my strength: whom shall I fear? The Lord is my light and my salvation; of whom shall I be afraid? The Lord is my strength: whom shall I fear?

Look up, Nora, roll your eyes, the upward ocular movement will help break the drug trance. This is why the psalmist says, Look up: I look to the mountains, wherein lies my strength. *Look up, Nora, look up.*

Yea, though I walk: get up, walk around. The Oche Nash, *Nora; you know it, I taught it to you. Say it aloud. God's love enfolds us, protects us. He will deliver us from evil.*

Alone, Larissa. Alone.

We are not alone, we are not alone, we are never alone, God is with us.

Nora heard Larissa as from a distance. "We are never alone," she mumbled. "But Larissa, we are. It's the nature of life, this loneliness. Kurt Cobain, David Foster Wallace, Primo Levi, Robin Williams, suicides. All the suicides."

"We are all alone here, dear Nora," Hawk replied. "You are all alone. All alone except for me. Think, Nora: Do you have any friends? Real friends? Would real friends let everything that has happened to you happen? And your colleagues—didn't they abandon you when you most needed them? How do you know they are not working for Ouspensky? You don't. No. Monstrous, really. No, darling, you really are all alone. Except for me. I love you. I am the only person in the world who cares for you now."

Nora's head nodded. Primo Levi. Auschwitz. If this is a man? The Chalet. God? No. Nod. Nap. Nothing else.

NORA, Victor Frankl! There is meaning in life. Nora, they can't take your soul, no matter how they try. Remember that. This next is going to be very ugly.

The door opened and Nora saw her mother, dead these 15 years, enter the room.

"Mama?" Nora whispered.

Mama smiled a crooked smile, showing her few brown teeth. She held a serrated 12-inch-long knife arced above Nora's head.

Hawk smiled. "Do you want me to tell her to leave?"

Yes, Nora shuddered, *yes*.

"Go!" Hawk commanded, and the ghoul left.

"Come here and sit on my lap," she invited Nora. "Good girl. Now I'm going to give you some love. Come to Mama."

***

CIA Director Andrew Franz and FBI profiler Audrey Uhuru surveyed the wreckage of Nora's apartment. Their sturdy shoes crunched broken glass as they went to survey the bookshelves where she kept her journals and poetry notebooks.

"I know what her casebook looks like; I think this is it." Audrey picked up a black-and-white elementary student's notebook. *Casebook*, it was labeled.

"She always took too many cases," Andrew grumbled. "We have to find her; I need her..." He stopped himself. "We need her to tell us why these creatures are circling her building."

Audrey smiled. "That's okay, Andrew; I love her, too." She opened Nora's casebook and a sheet of yellow 11 x 17 paper fell out. Audrey read.

"Holy shit," she muttered.

"What is it?"

Audrey handed the lined notes to Andrew.

The top of the list was obscured by a large coffee stain. The rest was scrawled in Nora's terrible handwriting:

My fuck list (in progress; convert for Sex and Love Addicts sex inventory).

Andrew paused, and despite his better judgment, read.

FUCKS

The Armenian bishop

Male prostitute from COWBOYS and Cowgirls bar

Ukrainian dwarf

My SLAA sponsors (3)

Sarah, beautiful Sarah

Adorable cross-dresser (when was this?) Blue eyes, Revlon red lipstick. Absolument charmante!

The four male transvestites when they were the towering geishas at the (year?) New York Halloween Day parade, and then again next year when they were the stewardesses. Tall men in platform heels, giant. Magnetic, totally irresistible.

Would-be warlock (Chris?)

Brave Mc Mcq.

Peter Cucumber (dead)

Robin Byrd dancers (14)

Too-wet Ava (what was I thinking?)

Cab driver #1; Cab driver #2; Cab drivers #1 and #2 (together)

Ah, the poets. Lovely. The one whom I let believe that he had taught me face and was so happy.

The poet Robert who lived near Cunningham Park—nice guy, funny.

The Russian poets (Stepka; Vanya; Kolya; Andriusha; Sasha; Vitaly; Alexei; Fedya; Marina)

The scholars: Baraka (quantum gravity); Mitchell (Egyptologist, Napoleonic era); Soroff (in process of discovering a new element for his rocket fuel); Mohammed Hussein (Roman Jacobson); Ng (Elizabeth Barrett Browning); C. Jones (GUT Theory); Tubman (Dickinson); Gillespie (Pushkin); Douglass (experimental poetics); Semenov (Byzantine empire); Houser (translator and scholar, Old Church Slavonic and early translations of Bible directly from Hebrew into Russian; see "Translators" below); McGuire (Slavic linguistics); Jimenez (Joyce); Wzynkovic (pre-Columbian art); Abruzzo (Kruchenych); the others?

The translators TK

My professor of Dada and Surrealism

My professor of Tolstoy and Dostoevsky?

My calculus professor

My advanced physics professor

The Bakhtin guy

The Gramsci guy

The Madness and Civilization guy

The homosexual who told me that his fuck list went back to Walt Whitman (impressed me, didn't know at the time that he was aping Ginsberg)

The one who introduced me to Roland Barthes

The Yale Men's Chorus

Six photographers

The Marxist (depressing)

One of the heirs to the Proctor and Gamble fortune

A Getty

A Rothschild

Actors and actresses (list later)

The holographer Sam

The guitar players, rock, classical, acoustic OMG (24)

"But square-cut or pear-shaped, these cocks don't lose their shape, penis is a girl's best friend."

To be continued …

Andrew looked despondent.

Audrey looked at him with compassion. "Sex addiction is a disease, Andrew. A treatable disease."

Andrew exhaled deeply. "Let's look at the casebook." They sat down on Nora's battered couch. Huddling together, they read...

The Cult

John Lennon Strawberry Fields an orphanage unspeakable acts of pedophilia because "nothing is real, and nothing to get hung about." Following Yoko for leads; what was her part? Masochist, handler? Blindfolded on Instant Karma vid: What didn't she want to see? Johnlennondead girlsint heparkimagine Sharon the Dakota Rosemary's Baby Ouspensky there occult center for Cult the plaques on the benches around the Imagine circle, a cemetery, the bodies buried beneath there Ouspensky sells the plots. Trail of crack vials and cigarette butts at certain areas, stones, ritual altars? Follow the squirrels and the birds and the vegetation to find the bodies what does Yoko know? Chapman knew about the pedophilia? No, that's what they told him. Manchurian candidate.

Patti Smith participated in Ouspensky's Black Masses, putting a knife to a child's "smooth throat" and eating from his cranium.

I experienced the deaths of two young women in Central Park not my own

did I see is this a memory or another phenomenon

his scent?

I remember saying aloud "Genya"

after experiencing what I experienced I went to the back gate of the dakota trying to gain entrance the guard stopped me brusquely I think the name of one of the girls is Sharon I think two girls were raped and murdered in Central Park near the Imagine

a workingclasshero is it something to be? media hound yoko brought girls to him where did I hear that?The disturbing recording of what to me sounds like a Black Mass or satanic gathering at the end of the White Album the child the child crying

the dakota the scene of Rosemary's Baby. number nine number nine number nine numberninenumber who is number nine??????????????????????????

"John Lennon? The *White Album?* Patti Smith?" Andrew asked Audrey in disbelief.

"She realized, we the Ghostbusters realized, that she'd been duped, that this was an Ouspensky disinformation plot. Look here. I'll brief you later," Audrey replied. "This cult stuff goes deep." They read on.

This is a plot to take down powerful artists, Lennon, Patti, to discredit them, dupe them. They went to a lot of parties high. Parties I went to who was there?

The lobotomized Kennedy women. I'd rather have a bottle in front of me than a frontal lobotomy....

Ussasis, Jackie U, Genya squiring her around while Jack acted out as a speed addict, sex addict. Jackie, you should have gone to Alanon!

Track down the "Ghost Busters," the cops like Audrey who worked the early cases of ritual abuse and were Serpicoed for it, harassed, busted, who had the balls and vaginas to face up to powerful perps and try to take them down, at great risk and harm to themselves. Find them, get help. They have the stones.

I thought in 2006 that I had broken my conditioning; the latter through beeps and boops and all kinds of hoodoo. They have abandoned their petty tricks, upped the ante. Clang, clang, clang went the trolley....

This period (2003–2006) when my kundalini would rise

to the point that I could punch, hit, kick, run with such power and force: poisoning using Deal neuromodulators? Do I have a native imbalance of P-substance or has this been induced?

"P-substance?" Andrew asked.

"A pain neuromodulator," Audrey answered. "Let's try another journal." She opened another black-and-white school book.

For Thesis: Ritual abuse tactics are crazy-making. They are designed to confuse. These include harassments that result in time-consuming trips to rectify health and other problems. Leaks, broken wires, pharmacy screw-ups, problems in one's apartment, premeditated setting up of accidents. False charges, small (and large) attacks. etc. Frequent harassing telephone calls. Not difficult to implement, but resulting in exhaustion, depression, and hopelessness on the part of the target. These tactics overwhelm, so that the victim has difficulties performing work and self-maintenance tasks. They enervate, isolate, deplete savings and other resources.

With the help of drugs and imprinting of stimuli during altered states caused by terror, anger, and confusion, ritual abusers can program their victims to respond to sound cues, words, double-bind language. These cues for behavior are based on Pavlovian and Skinnerian conditioned reflex theories. The strongest and most effective conditioning is variable-reward conditioning [Skinner, which work?]. Rats run mazes better when they are variably, rather than reliably, rewarded [endnote]. Note slot machines, social media likes, the tenacity with which women attach to men who don't reliably call.

Conditioning begins very early in the lifetime of an abused child, who has no other context but the abusing environment and therefore no way of gauging the extreme abnormality, dysfunction, and cruelty of her or his abusers. The child may have difficulty getting outside support. Isolation is key to continuing abuse [note: Deal discouraging me from seeing friends and going to meetings]. Harassments, mental and physical attacks, and other cruelties and abuse are usually stepped up by abusers when the target reaches out for help.

Reasons for victimization include sexual exploitation like child pornography $$, sex slavery, incest. Abusers also are vested in keeping their target from reporting their criminal behavior.

Sociopathy: This troubling population, the "people constitutionally unable to be honest with themselves," as mentioned in the AA "How It Works"—I have read about them. They have not responded to talking therapy; better people than I have wrangled with them.

You don't talk to Satan. Exorcists, through the power of God, command the Devil to leave. It is God, and not the exorcist, who expels Satan.

Mantra and sutra as therapy for reinforced behavior. Meetings.

Limitations of the behaviorist model of human life TBD.

Punishment is not the opposite of reinforcement.

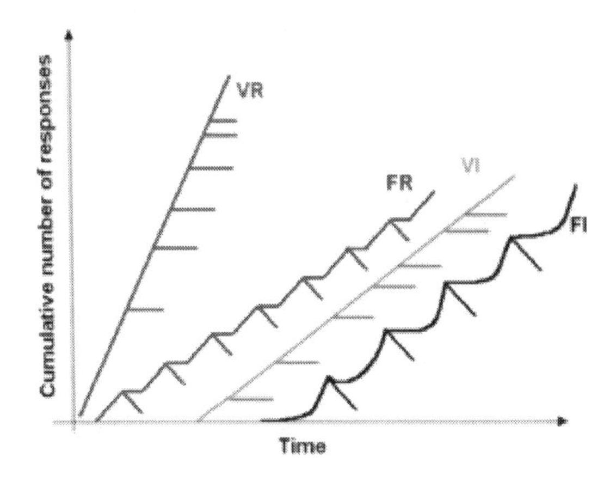

A chart illustrating the different response rate of four simple schedules of reinforcement; each hatch mark designates a reinforcer being given.

Leyton argues serial killers choose victims who originate from whichever class or group they blame for their presumed loss of power GET CITATION

Treatment of Sociopathy (for thesis intro)

The reported prevalence of sociopathy is [bet. 3—30? Check references and footnote] percent of the population. Indications are that this population is growing. This population, the "people constitutionally incapable of being honest with themselves," as mentioned in the *Alcoholics Anonymous* "Big Book" chapter "How It Works" [footnote], have been traditionally left unhelped by therapy.

Sociopaths are people, not Satan, and may be the loneliest people on Earth. Note F. Scott Peck's "evil" stalker in *People of the Lie* [Note]. The girl in question has affection only for some metallic object. It is my hypothesis that the worst sociopathic offenders, like the girl mentioned in Peck [Peck, 1], as children had consolation from abuse from no living thing—no person, no animal, not even plants, no organic life. As they were enduring barbarous abuse, inanimate objects such as a red wheelbarrow formed the only non-abusing objects to bond with. Imagine the substitution of maternal mirroring with a pair of scissors, a knife, or the child's own tortured image in a mirror

cutting my eyebrows off age 4

cutting my hair off

carving eyes on furniture crazy maternal eyes

OR KNIFE.

This is the ground of formation of the sociopath.

Treatment for sociopaths and psychopaths: singing, regression, mirroring [maternal and never sexual to avoid re-traumatization], finger painting, exercise, esp. dancing.

AA MEETINGS, SELF-NARRATION OF STORY TO AN ACTIVE LISTENER, POSITIVE REGARD

FRIENDSHIP

FORGIVENESS

TRUST

LOVE

SOBRIETY

Mama's hollow regressed-child voice happily saying, "Soup!" the only time I saw her genuinely happy; I need to see my parents and abusers as deeply abused children. Deeply abused children who identify [in many ways it is easier] with the oppressors, their abusers.

Even in the camps, girls fell in love and obsessed

about their Nazi infatuations, even to the door of the crematoria....

No.

No.

I can't do this.

No.

What about the victims?

the ring of children

Again.

When?

I run like a big cat through the park I am a huge predatory animal like a paleolithic cat I run through the bushes from 72nd street to there is a ball field an open area east of the road higher up 90th Street THERE it happened there

when the children were killed. Again.

Ouspensky singing everybody ought to have a maid I am Columbia the entertainment I sing they have me tied up my hands in the back and I get a hand free

I become banshee

buried alive someone scratching my head bringing me to consciousness swimming across the Hudson River

ring

fire

buried

heads

dead?

how old am I

?

infant toddler

When???????????? Time warp.

How often?

I am small then they don't kill me why

follow the $$$$$$$$$$$$$$$$$$$$$$$$$$$$$$$$$$
$$$
$$$
$$$
$$$
$$$
$$$
$$$
$$$
$$$
$$$
$$$
$$$
$$$
$$$$$$$$$$$$$$$$$$$$$$$$$$$

Stop. These are the people, to use the word broadly, you want to treat.

Why does everyone, including the good people of AA, think they are not treatable?

AND WHAT ABOUT THE VICTIMS? THE VICTIMS NORA YOU OWE YOUR ALLEGIANCE TO THE VICTIMS SERVE AND PROTECT…

No.

They have to be put down. It's the only way to stop them.

Genya. Genya. Genya.

NO! NO TREATMENT!

Even the peace-loving rabbis of the Warsaw Ghetto,

the God-fearing rabbis of the Warsaw Ghetto, committed to *ne soprotivlenie zlu zlom,* seeing the horror around them, seeing the deportations and murder, seeing the Nazis for what they were, irredeemably evil, even those good men stood up and said: GENUG! WE WILL FIGHT.

I am the Warsaw Ghetto.

Think about Genya in treatment, Nora. Think about it.

There is nothing but con there. Nothing. You think he loves you in some way. He doesn't.

There is nothing there. You can't imagine it because they fake it so well, but there is no human feeling there.

Interesting idea here about false identity, on a spectrum, in all of us, the ego as opposed to the true self. Survival identities shed in recovery to reveal true being and oneness with God. We are all false; who am I to judge?

No.

Is it evil to destroy evil?

You have to take him down. You may be the only one who can do it.

Breathe. Pray. Ask for strength from God.

My kundalini is rising. I am Don Juan Yaqui. I am calling the Holy Spirit to take me. I call on God to help me.

The Christ said very clearly that we could do what He did if we tried.

Faith. Unknown to Genya and his ilk.

I can do all things through Christ which strengthenest me.
I can do all things through Christ which strengthenest me.
I can do all things through Christ which strengthenest me.

I can do all things through Christ which strengthenest me.
I can do all things through Christ which strengthenest me.
I can do all things through Christ which strengthenest me.
I can do all things through Christ which strengthenest me.
I can do all things through Christ which strengthenest me.

My kundalini RIIIIIIIIIIIIIIIIIISEEEEEEEEEEEEEEEEEES

HEY, OUSPENSKY: I AM SMARTER THAN YOU NICER THAN YOU TOUGHER THAN YOU AND YOU DON'T REALLY LOOK THAT HOT ANY MORE (I'M SO SHALLOW).

AND YOU ARE BOOOOOOOOOOOOOOOOOOOOOOOOOOOORING GO TAKE IT UP THE ASS

I want you dead. I am more important and valuable than you. Intrinsically, not due to any special achievements; simply so. You are a predator and must be put down like a plague-carrying shit-covered rat gnawing on the toes of a child, like a blood-sucking louse. People must be kept safe from you.

I DON'T LOVE YOU ANYMORE. AS I SEARCH MY HEART I SEEK FOR SOME EMBER OF WHAT I ONCE FELT AND I FIND ONLY SORROW GRIEF DISGUST AND SHAME. YOU TORTURED ME. I DON'T HATE YOU. YOU SIMPLY MUST BE ELIMINATED TO KEEP PEOPLE SAFE. I CAN'T GRIEVE YOU AS LONG AS I REMEMBER WHAT YOU HAVE DONE. I AM SEEKING HELP FOR MY ADDICTION TO YOU SO THAT I DO NOT LAPSE INTO FANTASY AND A STUPOR OF NOSTALGIAC RECALL. I HAVE A LOT OF HELP IN THIS AND A VERY STRONG PROGRAM. AND I HAVE GOD TO HELP ME DO WHATEVER IT IS I NEED TO DO.

LET ME SPEAK HONESTLY NOW WITHOUT BRAVURA OR GAMES. YOU NEED TO BE PUT DOWN.

I CAN FIND YOU WHEREVER YOU GO AND WILL HELP THE POLICE DO SO. I CAN TRACK YOU. I KNOW YOU BETTER THAN YOU KNOW ME.

I WILL NOT ENGAGE YOU. YOU ARE A CRIMINAL AND I WON'T PRETEND TO UNDERSTAND THAT PART OF YOU BUT I AM LEARNING ABOUT SOCIOPATHY AND NEED TO SET THIS BOUNDARY. YOU NEED TO BE PUT DOWN.

I WILL NOT PRAY FOR YOU. I THINK OF THE HORROR PERPETRATED ON THE VICTIMS AND CANNOT.

I AM AWARE YOU ARE PREPARED TO KILL ME TO SAVE YOURSELF. I WILL USE EVERY MEANS TO PROTECT MYSELF. THE BEST MEANS IS THAT YOU BE PUT DOWN.

YOU HAVE USED YOUR INTELLIGENCE TO VICTIMIZE AND VIOLATE.

YOU HAVE USED YOUR GOD-GIVEN TALENTS TO SPREAD UNSPEAKABLE AND UNFORGIVABLE HORROR. I KNOW YOU WILL NOT STOP UNLESS YOU ARE STOPPED. I KNOW YOU WILL MURDER ME TO SAVE YOURSELF AS EASILY AS SWATTING A FLY.

AND IF I DO TAKE YOU DOWN OR RATHER, WHEN I TAKE YOU DOWN, IT WILL BE MORE GOD'S SUCCESS THAN MINE.

YES, I AM COMING FOR YOU.

YES.

I am Larissa Ekaterina Anastasia Nikolayevna Romanova, a lineal descendent of Catherine the Great.

I am the servant of the Most High Lord of Hosts, the Holy One of Israel, who, through his Infinite Grace, gives me the

Power to work His Will.

And you are but a henchman of the lord of the flies.

Do you dare to shake your puny fist in the face of God?

You do?

Ah, well then. You leave me no choice.

En garde. Prends garde, Ouspensky.

C'est à nous, Ouspensky. C'est à nous.

As Andrew stared at Nora's insane—how insane? he wondered—writing, a call came in. "The pterodactyls are moving, Dr. Franz."

"Dr. Uhuru," Audrey's phone spoke simultaneously. "The Aliens are moving east, copy that, heading for Queens."

"Copy."

Andrew tucked Nora's journals under his arm and he and Audrey left Nora's apartment. Clangs belatedly followed the friends.

***

It had been fairly simple for Michael to extricate himself from the dim-witted orcs, whom he threw into the furnace for the Sadie Ladies' Special now being hologrammed all through the Crematorium bowels, but he had to admit that he was getting tired. But he needed to get to Nora.

Conserving energy, he walked down the rectilinear corridors of the floor. He passed hotel rooms with suite numbers out of sequence, first 1500, then 1800, then 3, then zero. The effect was unnerving. He realized after a few minutes that he was in a maze

Don't look at the numbers, he told himself. *Something*

is weird here. Fly blind, his instincts said. *Shut your eyes.*

The elevator appeared as out of nowhere. Michael tried to activate it with a "Fuck off" as Ouspensky had, and couldn't. He paused to regroup and looked around. The numbers on the hotel suites throbbed and pulsed. He shut his eyes again. He couldn't believe what he saw in his mind's eye.

A fire escape! A fire escape in Hades! Hilarious, if he had the time to laugh, which he didn't.

Michael raced down 88 floors to the winding Escher steps at the entrance of Deal's lab. He opened a door on -300 with the YOUSUCK logo on it and found a monitor. Nora was responding to Hawk's "treatment." He looked away, boiling with rage at Hawk's molestation.

She's broken, he understood. He raced out of the monitor room and threw himself into the dozen orcs guarding the first circle. He briefly realized that he was killing men now and not girls; it felt more satisfying, somehow, cleaner.

Michael burst into Hawk's office and shoved the plate of macaroons into her face. He grabbed Nora and began the ascent up 300 flights. It took him 50 flights to realize that Nora, his Nora, was in his arms.

This is holding a real live girl, he mused. *This is much better than oatmeal. Even better than hot, if that were possible.*

Michael's energy surged and he flew up the stairs. But by -201, Michael felt his energy drain.

I can't carry her another two hundred flights, he realized. *We have to find another way.* He urged her to walk. Nora resisted.

"Not the Chalet, don't take me back to the Chalet,"

she repeated. She started to cry. Michael's heart broke.

She's delirious, poor kid. Michael stroked her hair. "Come on, sweetheart, you can do this," he urged. *Get her into a vacant room. Rest. Try again.*

Carrying Nora, Michael climbed the last vertiginous stairs to the -200 level and came to a floor with small gray apertures like windows. Mirrors. Tinny, some cracked. This didn't look like any part of the subterranean Crematorium structure. Where the hell were they?

Michael opened the only door. A bedroom, what looked like a dull and depressing nursery. A gray crib in the corner, a large bed in the center of the room. Toys in the crib, black and brown. The air suffocating. He laid Nora on the bed. Was this a hologram? No, tactile, real.

A rack of magazines. German. Michael looked at the dates. 1933, 1939. He leafed through them. Hitler in the park, Hitler with his dog, Hitler exercising. On the walls, shiny metallic objects. Knives, swords, scalpels, scissors. Who was, excuse the word, nurtured here?

Ouspensky. This was Ouspensky's nursery. Michael didn't know how he knew that, but was certain it was true.

The walls shuddered and disappeared, then reappeared. Windows! None of the other rooms had windows. Above them, Michael saw the parking lot of the Crematorium and the cop car he had stolen. Hope and relief flooded him.

Then he heard Ouspensky's voice. In his head. Laughing. A trap.

"Let's do the time warp again," Ouspensky cackled.

Suddenly, Michael heard aircraft. Real. He looked out the window. Reconnaissance craft, bombers heading right toward the crematorium. Could they see this room?

"Let's do the time warp again...," Ouspensky sang.

Voices of the bomber pilots. One of the pilots was saying Nora's name, ordering them to move in. No, they couldn't see her. But they knew she was there.

Nora came to life. "Andrew!" she cried, overjoyed.

Michael experienced another new feeling, in his gut and loins and burning his eyeballs out of their sockets. *WHO THE FUCK IS ANDREW AND HOW DO I KILL HIM?*

The planes were closer now, buzzing the building. The voices louder: "You wanna live forever, motherfuckers?" Andrew was shouting. "Move the fuck in." And then a pilot's voice in some kind of experimental craft that looked like the Birds … they had designed a plane based on the aerodynamics of the Birds.

They buzzed again. Crosstalk. The pilots were competing with who would spring Nora from the Crematorium.

The planes and the window abruptly disappeared. The nursery became a buzzing, vibrant network of tiny orange stars, pulsing and throbbing.

Michael heard Ouspensky laugh. "Your one-string brain cannot grasp the temporal dimensionalities of the multiverse. What you saw is what you so primitively call the future, what you can grasp of its Library of Babel combinatorics. Look well, motherfucker, it is the last thing you will ever see."

"Ho-hum," Michael answered. "Time is space and you think you can quark dance yourself into eternal life by bashing particles in the accelerators you control with your new laser." Michael pulled out his phone and tapped. He lifted the screen toward the brightest patch of stars. "Here you go, Genya, superstring for dummies."

String theories							
Type	Spacetime dimensions	SUSY generators	Chiral	open strings	heterotic compactification	gauge group	tachyon
Bosonic (closed)	26	N = 0	No	no	No	None	yes
Bosonic (open)	26	N = 0	No	yes	No	U(1)	yes
I	10	N = (1,0)	Yes	yes	No	SO(32)	no
IIA	10	N = (1,1)	no	no	No	U(1)	no
IIB	10	N = (2,0)	yes	no	No	None	no
HO	10	N = (1,0)	yes	no	Yes	SO(32)	no
HE	10	N = (1,0)	yes	no	Yes	$E_8 \times E_8$	no
M-theory	11	N = 1	no	no	No	None	no

[4] Wikipedia

Michael chortled. "Oh, wait!" he laughed a genuine hearty laugh. "*Deal* did the physics, right?"

The happy stars turned black. "I want the bimbo," Ouspensky said, barely controlling his rage.

"You can't have her," Michael replied simply. *And*, he thought, *if this jerk Andrew can get her out of here, he can ... what am I saying?* Michael asked himself in genuine wonder. *What am I feeling? I feel … what am I feeling?*

The photographer. The dumbass sweet photographer was in the quantum field with him, seeing what he saw, knowing what he knew, holding Nora.

Well, Michael thought pensively as his emotional world imploded, *I'm think I'm going to abreact now.*

***

Audrey and Andrew followed the Birds as they flew to Queens, leading the operatives to the Crematorium. At the Crematorium, the Birds stopped, hovering over the brick building. As they came closer to ground, Andrew saw and marveled at their size. He could see the folds of their leathery wings and their huge yellow talons and their strangely clouded white-blue eyes. Scored legs like chickens, except for the throbbing purple veins. Nora would say they were like Baba Yaga, fierce witches from another planet.

There was an unbreachable force field around the Crematorium. Audrey had contacted the best people for the case, physicists, scientists from Project SETI and the foremost linguists in the world, including Nobel laureate Aura Kenyatta Shevchenko, a double laureate in linguistics and theoretical physics. She knew Nora corresponded with Shevchenko and figured this would give them an edge in communicating with the creatures that seemed to have a special interest in her friend.

Audrey waved to the laureate, who had just driven up in a blue Lada past the rings of cops, FBI, and CIA agents surrounding the crematorium parking lot.

"Thank you for coming, Dr. Shevchenko."

"Call me Aura," the laureate answered, shaking Audrey's hand warmly.

Her bio said she was over a hundred years old, Audrey thought, appraising the older woman. *She looks seventy.*

"I have enjoyed my correspondence with Nora on Slavic linguistics," Shevchenko told Audrey. "She also sent me a lovely poem." Shevchenko lifted her elfin chin toward the sky. "This will be very, very interesting." she mused. She turned to Audrey and Andrew, who tried not to stare at the linguist's multiple facial piercings. "How can I help?" Shevchenko asked.

"Why are they interested in Nora?" Andrew asked. "Can you talk to them?"

"I don't know," the laureate answered. "Let's find out."

The Birds suddenly broke their holding pattern. With a metallic cry, they turned and formed a V in the sky. It seemed to be pointing toward Shevchenko.

"V formation is for travel among migratory birds. The cry could be group signal to start to fly," Shevchenko observed.

The Birds sang again, a short and punctuated cry. Shevchenko took a long, deep breath. "Yes?" she sang out toward the sky, mimicking the Birds' metallic tone.

The Birds answered immediately. Again, the tone was metallic and short. The laureate repeated her vocalization, louder and with more warmth.

Yes, the Birds replied. A longer, louder, happy *yes*. And friendly, like a gong or bell.

Friendly, but something else, Audrey thought. *Relief. They sound relieved. Is that possible?* She looked with awe at Shevchenko. *She's communicating with them.*

The laureate smiled, then frowned. She shook her small white-blue-and-pink-haired head vigorously side to side.

"No," she cawed.

A sharp metallic burst answered.

The laureate was grinning; she looked like she was having the time of her long life. She hopped side to side twice and then danced in a series of semicircles, bobbing her head up and down and flapping her arms. Andrew thought she had gone insane. Then Shevchenko stopped and turned to the Bird with outstretched arms.

"Hello!!" she cawed again loudly, waving and smiling and dancing. "Welcome!" She sounded like a demented crow.

The Birds emitted a series of long and joyous calls. The flock moved side to side twice, and then executed a series of turns, half-circling, flapping their wings gracefully and bobbing their heads.

Shevchenko laughed and jumped up and down. "Contact," she cried. "First contact! And I lived to see it!" She cawed "Hello" back enthusiastically.

Andrew stood staring with his mouth open. "She sounds exactly like them," he whispered to Audrey. "Who is this woman?"

Shevchenko collected herself. "Okay," she said to Audrey and Andrew, "We know how to say *yes* in their language. Greetings and courtesies are started. Next their names, then numbers." She turned to Andrew. "Have you recorded this?"

"Yes," Andrew stuttered.

"Your people can run some analyses of tone, pitch, timbre, duration, phoneme frequency?"

Andrew pulled himself together. "Whatever you need."

The Birds suddenly broke formation. They moved randomly, flapping their great wings, emitting rapid urgent cries, becoming louder and more insistent with each repetition. Then the Birds froze stock still in the sky above the amazed crowd.

"Danger," Shevchenko observed. "Imminent. Friends, let's go to it. We may not have much time."

"I'm afraid you are right, Dr. Shevchenko." The speaker was a tall man with long curly hair and a kind face, folded like a bloodhound's. He was wearing a large gray hat with a small red floral pin at the band. The worried mayor of New York was ordering him through the police barricade.

"Dr. Shevchenko, Dr. Uhuru, Dr. Franz," he nodded at the laureate and Audrey and Andrew, offering his hand to shake. "Bensinck. My name is Bensinck."

"Baron Batty Bensinck?" Audrey blurted out before she realized how rude she sounded. Was this the notorious and flamboyant peer of England she had read about in the tabloids?

The Baron smiled. "The same, Dr. Uhuru." His smile

vanished as fleetingly as it had come. "There is indeed very little time. Nora's life depends upon our expediency. I have information that may be useful to this case. May I brief you and Dr. Franz in my lab? It is a few miles from here."

The Birds emitted a long *YES* and resumed kettling.

Andrew looked to the sky and thought of Nora on ice skates. He was reluctant to leave the scene. How did they know the Birds were really protective of her?

Bensinck seemed to read his mind. "Dr. Franz, we need to learn more about these creatures. And we need your help."

Andrew nodded. The three and Bensinck piled into the Mayor's waiting limo and sped off.

***

Horror. Horror. Horror. The photographer stood at tbe brink of Michael's mind, knowing knowing gnawing. This isn't this can't this isn't me it is my my meeeeeeeeeeeee oowwwww aaaaaaaaaaaaaaaaaaaaaaaaaaaaaaay.

"Get out of here!" Michael commanded the photographer. *Me, that's me*, Michael realized. "Whoever you are, get out of here!"

The photographer/Michael stood corpse-still, a string of yellow vomit hanging from their chin.

"Listen," Michael began with all the force at his command, which was little. "This is not the time or the place to abreact. We have to get her out of here."

"Help!" the photographer screamed. "Help! Help! Somebody please help..."

"You can't help me," Michael insisted. "Go away. Go now!" Michael felt something wet on his face. He was crying—no, blubbering.

"You, you, you, I, weee ..."

Michael tried to tell the photographer to shut up. Instead, the image of his last kill, Susie, Susie, burned his or the photographer's—whose? his? mine? ours?—visual cortex to shreds.

"STOP!!!" the photographer was screaming. He was dizzy, puking, fighting with all his might not to know this:

A drummer. She told me in the car that she was learning to play the drums in her boyfriend's boy boy boy girl SAY AH LITTLE GIRL *band. I sneezed and she gave me she she she she she she Susie her name was Susie she had a name she gave she gave me* GIVE IN CUNT *her handkerchief, pink, with little red flowers. So young how young thirteen maybe, no more than thirteen Michael what have you done what have you done* I KNOW WHAT I LIKE I *she's God screaming* CHANTILLY LACE AND A PRETTY FACE A GIGGLE IN THE TALK I LIKE IT LIKE THAT *screaming screaming begging crying praying begging don't kill me don't kill me please I stuffed the handkerchief in her mouth you KNOW what you have DONE* I KNOW WHAT I LIKE *please don't kill me I'll suck your penis* HERE COMES THE BIG BOPPER BITCH *my skin don't cut my skin she's peeing crying your penis I know how please please don't* DONE.

The blood vessels in the photographer's eyes burst, leaving the whites scarlet. Michael wiped the vomit from the photographer's chin. With superhuman effort, he contained himself and banished the photographer.

STOP. IT'S JUST A KILL. GET NORA TO THE DOLL HOUSE. MORE FUN.

Michael looked at Nora, huddled in a corner. She had defecated and was playing with her feces. "Yoiya," she was saying gleefully as she rubbed her shit on the magazine stand.

She's shattered, Michael realized. *She's regressed to infancy. Poor thing, what have they done to her?* Michael felt a moment of deep compassion. He quickly squelched it. "No time for that now," he said to the photographer, who still lingered at the corners of his psyche. "We have to get her out of here. There are no planes or Andrew out there, and he can't help her, but I can. Breuer. Freud. DID treatment techniques. Will read." He looked over at Nora again. She was eating her own shit.

Michael was paralyzed with sorrow. *How do you I integrate her, abreact her, when I have done such …*

NO FUCKING TIME FOR THAT NOW. IT'S A GAME, AND I KNOW HOW TO PLAY IT. NORA WILL BE MY FIRST LIVE DOLL. I WILL BE THE PHANTOM OF THE OPERA AND WILL KEEP HER FOR MYSELF, TRAIN HER, DRESS HER, FEED HER. AND SHE'S MY FUCKING TOY, OUSPENSKY. MINE. I'M TAKING MY NORA DOLL TO THE DOLL HOUSE AND SHE WILL LIVE WITH ME FOREVER.

The quantum field shuddered. "You're trapped," Ouspensky sniggered.

GO FUCK YOURSELF, YOU OLD FART.

Michael surveyed the orange quark field. *Okay, this field is reality*, Michael figured. *But the ordinary mode of perception still obtains. Let's look at it that way.* He concentrated. "There," Michael said to Ouspensky as the nursery reappeared. Michael shook his vomit-covered, bloodstained head in amazement. *He really is an asshole, this prince of Nora's.*

Michael looked outside the window, which had reappeared. There was the cop car he had stolen, a few feet away in the parking lot.

"You can't get out." Ouspensky sounded unsure.

"Watch me," Michael replied. He grabbed Nora and jumped out the window, landing like a cat on his feet. Covered with Nora's shit, he carried her to the cop car, threw her in the backseat, and drove off.

What the hell does she see in that idiot? he wondered as he steered back to Manhattan.

***

Bensinck's lab was an enormous yacht the size of an aircraft carrier anchored in New York harbor; Audrey remembered that it was the largest yacht in the world. Bensinck led Audrey, Andrew, and Shevchenko to what appeared to be an equally enormous crime lab.

Andrew marveled at the sophisticated equipment. "Even we don't have this stuff," he remarked grudgingly to the Baron.

"Our team has had some breakthroughs with lasers," Bensinck replied modestly.

"So has Ouspensky," Andrew retorted.

Men and their man caves, thought Audrey.

Bensinck ignored Andrew's hostility. "Let me show you some of Nora's writing we have been analyzing," he continued. "She's been on Ouspensky's tail, if you'll forgive the double entendre, and there is a lot to sift through."

Bensinck led Andrew, Audrey and Shevchenko to a theater. He activated a large screen. Andrew recognized Nora's horrible handwriting.

"That's the poem Nora wrote for me!" Shevchenko said proudly. Andrew read the words on the huge screen, not quite understanding them.

YOUR PROBABILITY AMPLITUDE

I glance and
a boson blinks
into view.
A strong force
beckons
even as
a weak force
radios decay.
The gravity
of the situation;
the magnetism:
I observe and
my attention
turns particles into power
tracks into trails
whims into waves.

"Actually," Dr. Shevchenko . . ." Bensinck began.

"Aura," the laureate prompted.

Bensinck smiled. "Aura," he said gratefully. "It was

actually originally dedicated to Stephen Falcon."

"Ah," Shevchenko smiled. "I knew she had a crush on him ever since he published *Z Theory of It All.*

"And," Bensinck continued, "Ouspensky before that. As were these."

A series of poems with scansions, diacritical marks, and underscores appeared on the screen. A voice synthesizer, sounding very much like Nora, read the words.

VOW
(for Genya)
\ / /
We will love like dogwood.
/ / (cretic)
Kiss like cranes.
Die like moths (cretic repeat)
I promise. (amphibrachic inversion)

JAMAS VOLVERÉ

To touch the sidereal limits with the hands—Otero

/ / / / (redo in trochaic pentameter)
To see you is to see a warm brown bird
flash in a black night: I shudder.
Gone are the stars that are not the sun
that punctuate heights no longer heights,
heights become space. Things I will never know
with my proximity senses are gone, all gone:
I will never hear a star upon this earth,
but I feel the warm gusts your wings stir up.
If in the daytime I were to leave bread and fruit for you,
you might come again. I am not so different from
the mangrove swamp where you play.

FOR SIX MONTHS WITH YOU

For six months with you, I would
Quit my lover (trochaic)
Leave the city
Sell my books. (/ u/ (u))

For six months with you, I would
Live in Kansas
Join a carpool
Shave my legs.

For six months with you, I would
Be an actress
Wait on tables
Burn this poem.

But what if it doesn't work out?

If it doesn't work out I'll join a convent
If it doesn't work out I'll cut my hair
If it doesn't work out I'll leave the country
If it doesn't work out I still don't care . . . .

For six months with you, I would
Break the true law
Break my poor heart
Break my vow.
Now ask me what I'd do
For a year or two.

"That's not bad, for poetry." Andrew exclaimed.

"Not bad at all," Bensinck agreed. "Nora dedicated and rededicated her poems multiple times; a bit disingenuous, but not unlike her idol Pushkin. She also dedicated them to a man named Bost."

"Niels Bost the serial rapist?" Audrey cried. *What had her friend gotten into now?*

"Yes." Bensinck's lip curled in distaste. "She calls him Nilly or Big Thing. They had a nine-year relationship, most of it through correspondence."

Audrey collected herself. *Be professional now.* "Bost. Hardened serial rapist and murderer in the U.S. and Brazil, where boys and women think the six-foot-three-inch blond and blue-eyed killer is a god."

Andrew hesitated. "Also, former special ops." he added. "A crack sniper, one of the best. Knowledge of nuclear physics at a very high level."

"Exactly," Bensinck confirmed.

Audrey stared at the men. Shevchenko seemed lost in thought.

"High clearance," Andrew shrugged.

This is what happens when men run ops, Audrey thought. She made a note to herself to get promoted.

"I have a few of Bost's love letters to Nora—excerpts mostly," Bensinck continued. "Nora is not good at organizing her papers. He writes how she has 'rocketed him from doldrums.'" Bensinck smiled faintly. "Doldrums: a rather quaint word for a rapist." The smile vanished. "Bost is married to a woman in Pennsylvania."

"I didn't know that either," Audrey said.

"I'll send you the files." Bensinck pointed to a chart

on the screen. "Note that his rape and kill rate did not go down while he was with his wife, but that there are no kills or assaults while he was corresponding with Nora. She really is the cure for sociopathy, as her incompetent therapist posited."

"How do you know about Deal?" Andrew asked defensively. "Nora is my case," he muttered to himself.

"I bugged his office," Bensinck replied. "I have been following Nora's case for many years."

"So have we," Andrew retorted. *Who was this guy?*

The Baron again seemed to read Andrew's mind. He let down his suave pose. "I was haunted by my inability to save the young Nora in a chalet in Mont Blanc. Here is the dossier."

Audrey, Shevchenko, and Andrew scanned the briefing papers and wept openly. Bensinck waited, and then spoke. "Unfortunately, my friends, we don't have time for the grief this horror requires. I, too, cried hysterically for weeks and was inconsolable. I hired a team of detectives to track her, protect her. I tracked her to the Swiss school and had her followed in New York. I walked down the street where she lived every day for years, hoping to catch a glimpse of her. She became a detective. I saw her apparently happy and unaware of what had transpired and decided that that was for the best. I continued to maintain a small army of people to guard and protect her for many years. Nora was oblivious of this."

Audrey shook her head vigorously, moved by the Baron's vulnerability. "No, Nora often told me about her feeling of eunoia those days, that strangers around her were caring for her and protecting her in her building and on her block."

Bensinck continued. "I became obsessed with taking down Ouspensky. I built laboratories in my mansions in London, New York, and Paris, and here, seeking revenge for Nora and her children." He smiled. "I suppose I think I am Batman."

"Children." Andrew suppressed the urge to scream, shout, kill. "I never knew."

"I will brief you fully, Dr. Frank."

Andrew hesitated again. "Thank you, Baron," he finally said.

The Baron smiled a wan smile. "Albert, Andrew. Please call me Albert."

"Continue," Audrey urged.

"I have attended dozens of Ouspensky's Black Masses as a partygoer. I spent lavishly, and Ouspensky has not suspected me, although I have blown my cover now. I have collected very good intel on him, and films, which I will share with you. I have been in the Crematorium and know its layout." The Baron blushed slightly. "I have been able to rescue over three hundred victims from these orgies," he added modestly.

Audrey grinned at the Baron. *If I were bi, I'd ask this guy to marry me*, she thought. "You are not the Baron Batty, my friend," she told the Baron. "You are the Scarlet Pimpernel!"

The Baron blushed crimson. "Let me return to Bost and why he is important to us later. He may be able to help us."

"What!!!" Andrew and Audrey exclaimed simultaneously. Shevchenko absently nodded.

"Nora rejected Bost's proposal of marriage and urged him to stay with his wife. He came to hate her, a love-hate relationship, and his kill rate skyrocketed in Brazil and especially near Reading in Pennsylvania."

Andrew and Audrey nodded. "I remember those cases," Audrey said. "Does Nora know about his kills?"

Bensinck's lips curled peculiarly. Hatred and a trace of fear passed over his face.

"She does now. She may have suspected him before. Our Nora has strange taste in men." The Baron composed himself. "Bost is now in the hire of Nora's family, who are in turn in the hire of Ouspensky."

"Her family?" Andrew sputtered in rage.

"Yes, mother and father and niece. The latter was murdered, as was, apparently from these writings, her first husband. These seem to be a combination of notes for a story or film treatment or book of poems, or a diary. They are highly autobiographical, but with elements of fiction. She calls her protagonist Nora. Bear with me as we go through this background material, for it is critical to the understanding of Nora, her parentage, and these Birds."

Bensinck waved his hand and the screen came to life.

"Here is the introduction. It is unfinished; it seems to be in the style of an epic poem in bad dactylic hexameter. It looks like part of a separate work she tacked on to the treatment. There are also photos."

The screen shuddered. Images of mass graves, boxcars, an enormous concentration camp, what Andrew recognized as the Dora-Nordhausen complex in the Harz mountains, the Nazi's V2 factory, flashed before them, and then, in Nora's handwriting, a verse in poor scansion followed by photographs.

Dora, Verse 1

"'. . . and then the icepick broke, ha ha ha!'"
—Richard Pryor, "Mafia Club"

/ / / / / /
Sing, bride of Ares, of crimes once committed by banal, plain people, like
/ / / / / /
gangsters who torture and maim, and then tuck their small children in
without qualm:
/ / / / / /
Eichmann, so typical, could, would not, even at trial, understand what he
/ / / / / /
did wrong. And Mama and Papa, survivors of four camps: no traumatic
/ / / / / /
stress. They just spoke of days when they were young: Kalinivka, and how
they first
/ / / / /
met, not the flowering graves there of Jews, those mass graves; Przemyśl, the
/ /
scarce and spoiled food, but not
/ / / / / /
boxcars filled, bound for far ghettos; Erfurt, where the finest brick crematoria,
/ / / / /
sturdy, were built. And then finally, Harz mountains, Nordhausen, where

/ / / / / /
military V2 rockets were built; in the center, camp Dora, where
/ /
Jews and tired prisoners got gassed.

An image of Ouspensky's Crematorium, three-dimensional, rose on the screen. The caption, in Nora's handwriting, read:

Caption 1: Photo of the Fresh Pond Crematory in Middle Village, Queens; my parents moved near here when I was one.

The modern-day crematorium was followed by a similar and older image.

Caption 2: Photo of the crematorium at Dora Nordhausen (also Mittelbau Dora, Dora Mittelbau)

"Here, this will help you follow the writing." Bensinck distributed folders of scrawled text interleaved by typed transcriptions of Nora's micrographic handwriting. The words appeared on the screen punctuated by a bouncing-ball marker. A voice synthesizer read them aloud.

Thinking that your mother was an infanticide, that it is possible, is a difficult position for a daughter, it began.

Interlude: The Kapos

Plot line: Open medias res in 1990, with young Nora, 24, standing on the roof of a Harlem tenement singing "The Battle Hymn of the Republic" as Odetta sang it, at the top of her lungs—and her huge voice carries across the caverns from East 116th Street almost to the building she is fixated upon in the downtown distance, its neon crown blinking Satanic red, *666*, Top of the Sixes. She is mad, crazy like the fox, a woman whom a river of men will remember for the rest of their lives, a white woman with a fierce heart and steatopygous ass.

We see her having sex on the rooftops, picking up men in bars, walking from Harlem to the East Village, catcalls and propositions following her.

Scene Two opens to a festive dinner in the 1960s at the Alexenko family home; present are Leda and Nikolai Alexenko and their small extended family; the children include Nora, three, and Toma, eleven, and four cousins aged variously in between. The table is middle-class and abundant and after dinner, everyone plays cards. The men drink; the women serve them, and, as the evening wears on, the women chide the men for drunkenness, become angry at their mates and demand to go home; the men appease and laugh and cajole: just one more. This is familiar and expected. There is loud talk of "*the* war," the only war for the Alexenkos and kin: World War II.

The men play general, arguing how the war in Europe should have been prosecuted; the women talk of the children. (Should be reminiscent of *The Godfather*; the movie is the Ukrainian *Godfather*, as intricate and political, except here the Mafiosi living double lives are the Ukrainian Nazi collaborators, living and prospering in the United States. This is revealed through the course of the film, as are the crimes of Nora's parents, their atrocities, and later, black-market and other illegal activities post-war in the displacement camps—child porn, murder, blackmail, and bribery.)

NOTE: Leda tells her war stories in starts, episodically, never chronologically or sequentially. Nora once believed this was a function of traumatic memory. Now Nora knows Leda was covering things up and leaving things out.

THE UKRAINE, 1937: The Stalinist purging of Nikolai's father, taken away in the dead of night and no word for months; then, on the prison lines, his mother, Praskofia Femia, given his shirt with bloody bullet holes, and advised: *Move away from this town, remarry.*

Nikolai, a spoiled brat with a chauffeur and a car in a town with no other, respected due to his father's high official position as an undersecretary of agriculture in a country of agriculture, the country of the *chernozem* black loam known for its fertility and yield: the Ukraine, the bread basket of Europe, before the *kolkhozy* came. ("We are for the *kolkhoz*, but not in our village, quipped Leda often in the mincing voice of a *Reader's Digest* anecdote).

Nikolai was in college when all the other men were at the war, drinking and drinking and pawning his coat for drink and passing out on the college steps. Handsome and tall and steely-blue-eyed, chasing the girls or rather, being chased, like the only rooster in a chicken coop.

Then his father was purged, and he was now *sin vraga naroda*, son of an enemy of the people, left to take care of—his worst fear, to be responsible—two younger siblings and a mother (she remarries, letting Nikolai off the hook).

THE UKRAINE, 1943: Nikolai is denied a commission in the Red Army. He is a common soldier, this man who thinks himself uncommon; he is wounded and hunted by the Germans. Hiding in a cornfield, realizing he could die, 19-year-old handsome Kolya thinks: "Me … *me*! *I* am going to die!!!" But he survives and makes his way home.

He fights the German stragglers along the way and finds shot a German man, *a man like me*, he thinks, *with a picture of his wife in his wallet, and why fight him*? he asks himself. And the war continues and the Soviets lack ammunition and tell him to fight at the front without a gun and he says, fuck this! Leda's mother, wife of a prominent Ukrainian nationalist and Nazi sympathizer, has a friend among the Germans, a Ukrainian collaborator, and she asks them to take Nikolai, whom her daughter fancies. He is a mechanic, she tells them—they needed mechanics—and the Germans take him.

FLASH TO THE FUTURE: Nikolai shaking his head at Nora's left-wing politics: "I fought the Communists, of course you are a communist.…"

Nora remembers, cannot forget: She applies for a job with Nazi hunter Ely Weiss's foundation as a grant writer, and is interviewed by Mrs. Weiss. Nora hands Mrs. Weiss her poem, "How My Family Survived the Camps":

How My Family Survived The Camps

Was micht nicht umbringt, macht mich starker:
What does not kill me makes me stronger.
Nietzsche said this about other things
Not this.

How did my family survive the camps?
Were they smarter, stronger than the rest?
Were they lucky?
Did luck exist in Dora-Nordhausen,
Auschwitz and Bergen-Belsen?

How did my family survive?
They were young, my mother and father, in 1943
Twenty years old when taken as slaves.
No one knew my father was a soldier, a communist
So, he was not shot
Or taken to be gassed.
My grandmother said quickly to the Germans
He is a mechanic; they needed mechanics
My grandmother, Soviet businesswoman
Begged and bribed the Ukrainian *kapos*
Begged and bribed the Germans, not SS.
They took my father, son of a commissar
And shot the other men.

How did my family survive?
They offered no resistance
Did they collaborate?
Is complicity possible without choice?

They marched to Germany, working
Following the German army
Following the front
Digging trenches, carrying metal
These were the good camps, Kalinivka, Przemyśl
There was still food:
My mother recalls eating an entire vat of potatoes
Fouled by kerosene, discarded by the Germans, not SS.

The treatment was not cruel, comparatively, not cruel:
In 1944, the Germans
Were as afraid of the Russian front
As the prisoners were of Germany
And of the other camps.
Where they went nonetheless,
Where they were sent nonetheless.

How did they survive Erfurt, the selection?
My mother spoke good German:
I see her now at the staging camp
Her keen wit dancing around the SS
Like her young Slavic feet.
She was young and good-looking
Thin but good-looking
And the SS liked the Ukrainian Frauen.
On the cattle car to Dora
To the chimneys of that camp
My mother rode with her family intact
Thinner but intact
And ready for work.

How did my family survive?
Was it luck?
In Dora-Nordhausen
Where the air smelled of shit and gas
Where the sun rose but never shone
Was there luck?

The boxcar stopped
At the Nordhausen factory
The way out through the crematorium chimney in Dora
Here, my grandmother learned languages
Wstavach, Stoi, Ren, Schwein, Halt!
In Dora, where not to understand an order meant death
My grandmother learned six languages; after six months
My family could work, hide and ask for bread
In all the languages of Europe.
They learned English the same way.

How did my family survive?
When the Americans came, with chocolate and blankets
My father, six-foot-one
Was one hundred and twenty pounds
And still we were rich, my mother interjects,
Rich compared to the Jews.
A few months longer, though, a few months longer
We would not have been alive.

How did my family survive?
My grandfather, a teacher
Told this story:
When the Americans came and saw the camp

They invited the people to loot the nearby towns
Take anything, the well-fed soldiers said.
My grandfather stood and spoke: We are not animals,
he said
But we were, my father interrupts, we were.

How did my family survive?
Survive is not the right word.
I'm alive, my father would say, alive
Alive because I did not die; others died.
Keep breathing, he encouraged me in difficult times,
Keep breathing.

Mrs. Weiss leaves this unread. Looking at Nora like a prokaryote on a slide, she asks: "If your family was not Jewish, what were they doing in the camps?"

What? Bimbo, thought Nora, *unaware of the Slavs, gays, mentally ill, Russian POWs interned and gassed in the camps. How could this idiot woman be married to Weiss? Weiss, the Nazi hunter, obsessed and enraged and monomaniac, would see all Ukrainians as evil, as they weren't, as they weren't, as some were....*

But the poem had lacunae carved out by Leda's lies, Leda, head of the Frauenblocken in Dora, and Nikolai, risen from mechanic to *kapo* to trainer of *kapos* in the Nordhausen complex. And Nora was turning her family in, ungrateful snitch that she was. As her mother always said, she was kind to strangers, the little bitch. Like the model Soviet children who turned their anticommunist parents in to Stalin. Snitch-bitch. Telling the family's secrets ...

GERMANY 1946: After the war, in the displaced persons camp, Leda, a Ukrainian Medea, murders her two-year-old son Vova, the child she carried in the barracks of Dora-Nordhausen, to spite her lover Nikolai, who has lost interest in her, and because, at heart, she doesn't like children. This is not done impulsively, in a rage; Leda has much invested in being thought of as a good mother and knows that the death of a child will not reflect well on her, but her desire to be free of child care and her anger at Nikolai keep her focused on the slow poisoning of her infant. The child sickens; a Ukrainian quack is brought in to look at the miserable little boy and pronounces an ordinary stomach ache. Leda knows, when Vova is dead, that there will be no autopsy for a child of displaced camp persons; she also knows the camp doctor is incompetent and will diagnose whatever she suggests.

Leda is terrified when Nikolai, grief-stricken at the sight of his dead son (but too busy drinking and chasing his new squeeze, the Jewess Maryusya, to notice the child's illness before) bears his dead son to a German hospital. But a nurse looks at the dead child and coldly states, with a reproving *tsk* in her voice: "Only 1 in 10,000 die that way." (Note: roughly the statistics for infanticides.) She pronounces him dead of appendicitis, and Leda breathes a sigh of relief. Adopting the air of intense grief, which is fed by her anguish over Nikolai's affair, Leda spends her days at the child's grave, beating her head against the wooden Orthodox cross, a bloody welt on her forehead as a badge of mourning. Even so, now the image of maternal grief, somehow, she is still not the center of attention nor the focus of much pity. She is largely disliked by the other women, and attracts none of the men, including Nikolai.

Nikolai does not return to her, fascinated by the independent and spirited Maryusya. Nikolai's stern mother, a giant of a woman as tall as her six-foot-tall son, orders Nikolai to return to Leda, even though she dislikes her daughter-in-law. Leda tells the story, embellishing and rewriting history, as follows:

"Praskofia Femia looked at Nikolai and said, 'Nikolai, throw the garbage out.'"

And, obediently, Nikolai turned to Marusya and said, shrugging sheepishly, "Leave."

BROOKLYN 1966: In the United States, Leda reminiscences and smiles, transported to the camps where she translated, was important, a real translator, she said, not like the other Ukrainian women who were just whores; she smiles and speaks of the Jewish women in the Dora Frauenblock, who respected her. Nordhausen, the "good camp," Nordhausen and not the DP camp, where Nikolai left her for another, the good camp Nordhausen, where she would cry sweetly to her lover, Kolya, Kolya. . . Nikolka; and then stridently: Nikolai! and then furiously: Nikolai, *chorto-krokodil!* Laughing to herself, she forgot that Nikolai, busy with the hungry Jewesses, never came.

In the New World, in the Williamsburg slum, Leda conceives Nora with the last sex she will ever have. She eats so much during this pregnancy that she shocks her obstetrician with her weight gain; he tells her to stop eating so much. Leda finds a new obstetrician and acquires gestational diabetes. Later she would smilingly tell Nora, but not joking: "You gave me diabetes. "And:

"You made me lose my figure." Unspoken: *You made my husband stop loving me.*

This thought intensifies over the years. As an old woman picking at her warts, Leda broods on it: *You made him stop loving me*, nurturing in her murky, unexamined soul this deep resentment against Nora: *You made me lose the love of my husband*—forgetting she had never had it.

For this reason, Leda resents her youngest daughter, who loves but equally dislikes her mother. Leda is rough with the infant when no one is watching. Leda attends to Nora's needs angrily, and gives the child small quantities of vodka to make her sleep. Her husband Nikolai, returning home from "work," the ostensible overtime that Leda knows, in her heart, is time with women from the bars, the dark lean Jewesses her husband favors, adjures her to "play with Nora"; drunken and playful Nikolai loves the small Nora, who dotes on him. But sober, Nikolai is taciturn and withdrawn, and ignores and rebuffs the confused child.

Leda is tired of childrearing, despite the help of her mother and father who live with the Alexenkos. She wants a life, but can't get one, and wants Nikolai to love her; Nikolai is bound to her, but is chronically, persistently unfaithful and shuns Leda's bed. Leda stops breastfeeding Nora at six months, since the child objects to her rough, smothering, and hurried feedings, but Nora is not ready to be weaned, even from this callous mother. Leda gives her a glass to drink from instead, spiking the milk with vodka.

Bensinck suddenly stopped the projection.

"Have they made any headway on the force field?"

Audrey shook her head. "It is some new laser phenomenon. But the element powering is unknown."

The Baron came to life. "My scientists can help you there. Give them clearance."

"Done," Andrew said.

The Baron nodded pensively. "I've found that deep background is critical, especially in critical times. Will you bear with me to follow through the rest of Nora's writings?"

"Yes, yes, of course," Andrew and Audrey said simultaneously.

The screen shot to life, showing a child's drawing entitled *Chuchelo, Scarecrow.* It depicted a thin scarred terrified child in a straw crib; around her drunken Ukrainian people dancing lasciviously, smoking, setting the straw on fire.

QUEENS 1958: Leda's father, Nora's chief caretaker, has a stroke; Leda takes care of him a little, but leaves most of the work to her mother, Nora's Baba Nata. Nora, the infant, is abandoned. Still, Leda must attend to the child sometimes; often, when the child is sleeping, she stands over her crib, tucked into a corner of Leda and Nikolai's bedroom, holding a pillow. She thinks how Nikolai does not touch her these days, even drunk, and blames the needy child for this, and she stands with a pillow over the child in the crib, thinking, thinking hard. But two infant deaths would look bad, the canny Leda knows. But she is tempted, so tempted....

Bensinck waved his hand. A voiceover announced "Nora's juvenilia."

Love Is Blue

I remember my father's green Ford shaped like a pig
I remember Dyadya Esprokofim his body like a rooster big stomach veiny legs he owned a gas station people left dogs there
I remember Esprokofim fixed a car with a potato he sliced it thin and put it on the radiator he survived four camps my mother explained
I remember I had a rooster named Happy
I remember Tetya Ida Espokofim's wife she was thin Esprokofim liked my mother she was fat
He is not your uncle my mother explained he is my *cum* your sister's godfather I am his *cuma*
I remember I had a hamster named Happy
I remember Esprokofim driving to the beach buying us food hot doggie he would say hot doggie you wannit hot doggie?
I remember the ring of men
I remember Tetya Ida said that Mama had a son Vova died in Germany she banged her head on the grave every day until it bled
I remember Vanya Vanya the junkie Tetya Ida's son Esprokofim used to beat him he took me to the woods wrote my name with a stick run away he whispered run away
I remember the klieg lights the camera and the klieg lights and the ring of men watching
I remember Esprokofim was a kapo Ida said it Papa heard her he put his hands on her throat for a very long time then let go

I remember my father smoking in the basement lying on the couch and staring at the ceiling
I remember when my aunt Vera killed herself she jumped from the window her apron got caught in the telephone wire it hung from the cable for months
I remember my father called me “troublemaker”
I remember my mother putting things in my mouth keep quiet she said just stay calm
I remember the men I am in a garage there are ants there are men I am covered with ants on the ground
I remember the knots in my shoulders the hands in my back pushing down on my shoulders holding me still
I remember the smell of Lucky Strike cigarettes
I remember my jaw clenched my jaw tight a man pries my mouth open pours water on my head I open my mouth
I remember my mother standing over my bed she is holding a pillow she is thinking thinking hard
I remember Vanya whispering to me whispering call the police call the police
I remember my father in the basement drinking and reading he looks up from his paper don’t blame me for your problems my dearest don’t blame me
I remember my mother’s eyes blank and empty are you sorry poor Mama are you sorry I ask and the dark insane eyes stare back I say please crazy Mama oh please crazy Mama please don’t go to hell
I remember Vanya screaming at Esprokofim you can’t do anything to survive you can’t do anything to survive sometimes you just have to die but I said oh no Vanya oh no Vanya I know what it is to want to live

I remember my father's green Ford Mama opens up the window look up she says look up
I remember Esprokofim's face in the window thin and pale my mother saying wave goodbye he sees you wave goodbye they don't let children into the hospital
I remember that I got my own radio that summer the number one song was *Love Is Blue*

NORA AS A TEENAGER: *Nora, the beloved*, says Leda in a sick, twisted, and envious voice. Looking at Nora and in the same sickly tone: *You have your father's eyes, your father's lying, lying eyes.* Leda pimping the unconscious and brainwashed Nora, schooling her to "never refuse sex to a man."

Nora telling her camp family history to a rough and rugged Hassid she had picked up, who fucks his *shicksa* rabidly, literally frothing at the mouth. This large and unkempt man is one of Nora's few repeat stands. Most men, after the first fuck, are put off by her angry intelligence, others dislike her obvious lack of preening for them.

Nora reflects on her uncle, Dyadya Volodya, and his cancer, in the brain, in his arm, on his lung, the results of a seven-and-a-half hour biopsy to come soon and likely spell the energetic 86-year-old's death. She thinks about his endless stories of the camps and World War II, of the time he spoke of the railway.

"The Germans, you know, thought we were *untermenschen;* you know what that means?"

Yes, nodded Nora patiently, smiling and thinking of *Onegin*: "When will the devil cart you off?"

"Your grandfather and I were going to go guard the railroad, but the Germans would not let us go alone. Because we were *untermenschen* . . ."

Railroad Germans Germans railroads and this was a high level of collaboration not enslavement and grandfather grandmother guarded the railroad

what was in the cars at the stations the Jews stripped and beaten by Ukrainian kapos these untermenschen *not trusted to guard materiel, but trusted to guard strip beat Jews separate them into those fit to work and those to be shot the youngest children and infants pulled shrieking from their mothers and sent to die as mothers screamed and wailed and then stood silent in fear of their own lives*

They guarded the railroads.

Lager Nyc

You, volunteer:
Reichsgeboren.
You choose to be here
Select.

You, volunteer:
You know the difference
Between cause and effect:
The people on the street
Are too stupid to have homes
Too filthy to wash
See them root through the garbage

Nicht essen aber fressen
Ni yest' a zhryat'
They deserve to be there
They deserve to be there
Select.

Concentrate:
See the dark people
Sitting in the cells
They deserve to be there
They deserve to be there
And the women of the *Frauenblock*
The *Fraulein* triple X
Control her, detain her
Pick her up
Select.
Cause and effect:
You know which is which.
Select.

You, volunteer:
We see you
On the job where you whisper
Half of what you think
And none of what you feel.

See the clock:
The digital tattoo says run now
Rush to the train the transport
Who cares who gets in

Who cares who gets out
Push into the car the transport
Who cares who gets home
Who cares who gets shot
Arbeit macht frei.
You choose this
You choose this
Select.

Hey, you, volunteer
We find ourselves together in the subway
The Grand Ka-Ze Zentral:
Here in *Ka-Ze*
Your face is not a face
Ni litso, a morda:
Your face is not a face
But a snout
We don't eat here, we devour
Nicht essen aber fressen
Ni yest' a zhriat

We don't give an inch
And we don't give a damn
Only weaklings fall to the tracks
God knows the difference
Between cause and effect.

The selection is over:
Look how it happened that you fell.
You choose this
You choose this
Select.

FLASH FORWARD: Nora felt a weight upon her and, simultaneously, a weight lifted off her. So, it was true, it was all true. She thought of the long gray braids of her Baba Nata, undone at night, and of those efficient hands braiding Nora's hair for school. And where had those efficient hands been, the talented violin-playing hands, the guardian of the camp rail station, where the Jews came in to Dora …

Nora had questioned, often, Leda's paranoia and xenophobia, how her mother, catching her talking to a friend, grabbed at the receiver, screaming, *what are you telling them, what are you telling them about us?* Nora had put it down to shame, a reflection on her mothering. And a life divided between Hitler and Stalin could make one paranoid. But now, there was this—that people, through Nora's chatter, might know the truth about the war and the camps, the kapos, the Ukrainian Guard.

Schweinerei

Get up, schweinerei, *my father says, waking us late.*
And at dinner, my dyadya, *talking drunk and loud,*
says that he and my dedushka *guarded railroads*
in the war. For the Germans. The railroads are old,

but this country is new: not the Soviet Union, I ask?
not wanting to know. Barely breathing: the world,
hard, atrocious, and cruel, falls into place.
And Babushka? Babushka *worked at the railroad, too.*

(I feel her hard hands braiding my hair, the stern lips
mouthing: zhid*). I remember my mother, seeking salvation*
at her grave, saying (but lying): "I once opened a gate."
The world falls into place. What was on those rails? Who?

And what did their guards do? Somehow, I knew, I always
knew.
Tonight, I hear my mother's reedy voice simper, singing,
Nach jeden Dezember ihr kommt ein Mai. *Her home of*
gemutlichkeit, *comfort without joy. Her love for the*

German tongue; how often she said "There were good
Germans, too." As Ukrainians, save the martyred few,
they were gvardia, kapos, *collaborators, too. Did they have*
a choice? Starvation in the kolkhoz, *bodies lying, dying*

in the streets, and only the Germans, said my mother,
protested Stalin's rape and collectivization of the
Ukraine. How much victim? How much volunteer?
Did my mama, my papa, my dyadya, *my* baba, *my*
Dyedushka
commit atrocities in the war?

In Kalinivka, the mass graves; my family was there.
In Przemyśl, deported Jews; my family was there.
In Erfurt where crematoria were made, my family was there.
In the Harz Mountains, Nordhausen and Dora-Mittelbau;

my family was there. What other families? Who survived,
and why? (There was no crematorium in Dora, my mother

lied.) In the face of starvation, of death, of Stalin's camps, tell me, you, well-fed and safe, judging me and mine: is there complicity when there is no choice? (Was there choice?)

The stories, the lacunae, the lies.
Now I know why I always felt like a Jew. O, Adonai, why?
Why these origins for me, why no orisons for me?
The dead are dead, but not within me, my
holocaust today, forever my bread.

Now Nora knew why she always felt like a Jew, rooted for the underdog, leapt to the defense of the weak and disenfranchised. It was pure self-interest, for she was one of them.

FOR TREATMENT: We will see how Nora gravitates to sociopaths as a result of this upbringing, and to those Eric Fromm called malignant narcissists: the rapist Bost, Ouspensky, her first husband in his attempted murder of her on her honeymoon (arranged with Leda for life-insurance money, but foiled by Nora's unerring instinct for survival) and in her treatment by the malignant narcissist John Deal. Fromm's treatment of authoritarianism (read, "bullies," as in Leda and Deal) and its connection to narcissism—the *really* malignant kind—will connect back to Stalin and Hitler.

Nora has what Deal called "indomitable will." Which makes her willful. We watch as she figures everything out, mourns, and keeps her sanity and integrity in the end. Amen.

VOICEOVER AND GUITAR RIFF

WARSAW GHETTO

I am the Warsaw Ghetto
I am the underground railroad
I am a hero
I am the people who sang songs
Who said the Lord's prayer and the *Sh'ma Yisrael*
As the Nazis led them to the gas chamber.

I am a five-year-old girl in Jim Crow Mississippi going
to school
I am Rosa Parks: I stand before the policeman
Before his club and his gun
And I say: no.
You can't have mine
No.

They tortured me and I confessed, I couldn't help it
They put electrodes on my—
And I screamed
I told them everything they wanted to hear
But I never believed them
I never believed their lies
I always believed in love
Could see, in the distance, the light
And wait—I know it will come
For help.

I am a survivor
Of Mama's torture
And Daddy's rape

At age one
Age two
Age three
And now

I survived the selfish fondlings
The inspection of my genitals
The picking, groping hands
The gangbang
The lies

I survived the prostitution
The mutilation and sedation
The betrayal and attempted murder of my soul.

Don't tell me there is no God.
Who else helped me?
It wasn't you.
I called on God to help me.
There was no one else:
No mother
No father
No teacher
No preacher
No Rabbi
No doctor
No friend.

My enemies were powerful
Like Hitler and the Ghetto
But I held out

And when I tried to collaborate, wanting to die,
When I tried to surrender
I couldn't do it.
I had to stand up
Had to fight
No matter how many times they
Knocked me down
Called me crazy
Made me cry.

In the Ghetto
In the sewers
There is a record
A diary like mine
Of people who fought
Of people who fought and loved
Of people who fought and won
No matter what anybody says.

End Interlude

Audrey wiped her tearstained face. "I knew Leda and Nikolai. I was there at dinner when Nikolai attacked Nora's boyfriend Armando, who was rich, pleased at needling and insulting the 17-year-old boy, a guest in his house, calling him 'a coupon clipper.'"

"As he might have said to me," Bensinck reflected. Audrey remembered now that Bensinck was heir to the Krupp-Thyssen fortune, armament suppliers to the Nazis, and unwittingly stared at the Baron.

Bensinck stopped the projection. “They are alive, you need to know. Leda and Nikolai are alive and know about the Birds.”

“No,” Audrey interrupted. “Leda’s been dead 15 years and Nikolai was incinerated in a fire.”

Bensinck shook his head. “Ouspensky has had some breakthroughs in cloning. He has the potential to create armies of these perps.”

Andrew was pensive, taking this in. “I need more background on them.”

Bensinck selected a file.

“Here begins the writing on the cult murder of Nora’s husband Steven and Nora’s first ritual abuse.”

“Nora has an FBI file on the murder,” Andrew offered. “We’ll share it with you. Albert.”

The burst of a true smile crossed Bensinck’s face. “Thank you … Andrew, if I may. Here is Leda’s first attempted hit on Nora,” he said, activating the screen. “Notice Nora’s first person in these accounts.”

Blood Wedding

Steven used to say that one would think that chess was an elegant and refined game; the reality in New York, Steven said, was that it was the province of hustlers and cons.

When we met, I went to his apartment, where stacks of books formed stalagmites and stalactites into pillars.

He told me I had once rubbed my crotch against him at while drunk at a party while drunk. After a year of dating. I suggested we should marry. He told me that that was "ridiculous." But after a phone call with my mother, he proposed.

When we decided to get married, Steven was on the phone constantly with my mother. Said, "If what she did was conscious, it would be criminal." Mama suddenly became observant. We couldn't have the reception before the wedding because it was during Lent. We decided to have a small dinner at the Russian Tea Room. Papa was delighted that Steven picked up the check. And as things turned out, they got most of their money back for the reception, planned after our "honeymoon."

NOTES: Ceremony of innocence—cult plans Steven's murder for money, his West 77th Street penthouse overlooking the Museum of Natural History, and fun. A gambler who ripped through his fortune in Atlantic City and the market, Steven is in debt, owes money to the mob, and is desperate. He agrees to murder me, to stage a drowning death due to faulty equipment while scuba diving, and plans this with Leda for a big insurance payoff. I am supposed to die, but with my instinct for self-preservation, I live.

BREAK IT DOWN:

Steven and Leda arguing—Steven wants to marry right away, Leda want to postpone—she is suddenly religious and says we can't have the reception during Lent. (Fishy thing #1)

Steven and Leda arguing and constantly on the phone (Fishy thing #2)

So—they decide to murder me for insurance money. If Leda holds the reception after the honeymoon, she saves money. (Thrifty.)

He asked me whether I was really a Russian princess—what did Leda tell him?

When Steven and I come to our honeymoon hotel in Cancun, the honeymoon suite is booked. There are no vacancies. Some cult game? Moving me to another location for the kill? Steven is hysterical. "Let's get out of here!" he panics, getting cold feet. I reassure him; a hotel clerk asks a couple to give a room to the honeymooners. And so, it begins.

On the day appointed for my death, he is preoccupied, moody, dark, resentful.

We find the scuba instructor, a criollo, with two Mayan boys as crew. He is in on it, and knows, unbeknownst to Steven, that Leda has hired him to kill both me and him. And we dive, Steven first, then the instructor, and then me. I suddenly feel uncomfortable and make the up sign to surface; the scuba-diving instructor tries to show me the beautiful fish on the reef; I insist, up! And I come up, gasping for air.

What is fishy #3—they don't dive for Steven—they postpone this—they go to "get help" which takes an hour getting to the hotel and back. No help is found. Stalling for time and getting instructions during which Steven's murder is completed and covered up.

And you borrowed money from the mob....them's the breaks, them's the breaks.

Asked to give Steven's insurance money to Nikolai and Leda, I won't: I want the money to leave home and have a life apart from the family. Leda is stunned; this might be the first time I have defied her in any substantial way. Leda's hatred of me deepens. Spurred on by some deep life instinct, I move away from Leda, knowing that I will die if I do not—and Leda does what she can to kill me.

I look for an apartment. I answer an ad for a studio share on 125th Street and Claremont Avenue. The share is a room divided by a sheet. The would-be renter says, "I am a financial analyst, but what I really want to be is a scuba diving instructor." (Fishy #4)

I stumble out onto the street, lurching downtown on the west side of Broadway. The tall crazy drug dealer from the coffee shop Steven and I frequented is standing on the corner of 120th Street. He points at me, a malevolent Quixote, and says in a stentorian voice—YOU KILLED HIM! (Fishy #5)

I find a small apartment, a share with an Israeli frotteur named Gershon. Drugged by Deal on the incredible cocktail of Halcyon, Xanax, Lomotil, antidepressant and Lithium, I go into a coma (Fishy #6). My father comes to pick me up when Gershon calls him, but doesn't take my unconscious form to the hospital (Fishy #7). They leave me unconscious at the top of the stairs to the basement, perhaps hoping I will fall to my death. My niece Tara takes my pulse and checks my breathing. "Nora is in a coma," she cries, to the apathetic response of my parents. She insists I get treatment and Leda and Nikolai reluctantly accede.

Bensinck stopped the projection. "Steven's father was mob-connected, knew Bugsy Siegel; Steven was desperate for money, a drug dealer, and gambler—he was in debt to the mob."

Audrey nodded. "And Leda played him."

Bensinck nodded in turn. "Exactly. And this was filmed in cinema verité for the amusement of the cult; the movie, edited by a prominent filmmaker, is called *Blood Wedding.*"

An urgent series of caws reverberated through the yacht.

"They're here," Shevchenko said. "I must go."

"Yes, you must." The voice was of a tall blond man with exquisitely sculpted musculature.

"Bost?" Dr. Shevchenko offered

"Bost. I'm here to help."

***

Realizing I would give Nora to another man if it would save her started my abreaction, Michael reasoned as he drove the stolen cop car to La Guardia Airport. *But I still wanted her for myself, which stopped it.* He screeched the car through a broken gate at the south of the airport and transferred Nora into a sack and then into a red Maserati parked nearby. He hoisted Nora into the back seat and headed toward a private helipad.

"Mr. Bundy," a security guard acknowledged as Michael carried the mail sack with the unconscious Nora toward his helicopter. "Shall I call the pilot?"

"No, Bill, I'll fly her myself today."

Michael continued his assessment of the situation as he took off. *Ouspensky's armies are coming for her, and will track her here. And I have to get her together before they do.* He placed the copter on autopilot and released Nora, who was drooling and mumbling *aah aah I have to aah aah.*

She needs to take a shit. Michael patted Nora's matted hair. "Sorry, darling, you will have to go in your pants. It won't happen again," he promised his vegetable love.

He shook himself. *How the hell did I get this paternal? Is this "normal" love? I'm not having any trouble keeping my mitts off her,* he noted. *But just in case: What should I do to contain myself around her? Pretend she is a kill? No, somehow, I am containing myself. Bizarre, the effect she has on me.*

He landed the helicopter on a building in Tudor City and carried Nora to a rooftop elevator.

The elevator opened onto a cavernous triplex apartment decorated with Rothkos, Byzantine icons, and first editions.

"Welcome to the Doll House, my dear," Michael said, laying her on a long, plush, white couch, immediately stained by contact with Nora.

As he changed into clean clothing, Michael dwelled briefly on the fantasy of making Nora one of his dolls, a Russian boyarina of the era of Peter the Great. *Snap out of it,* he commanded himself. *But a change of clothing is in order. What won't stimulate me? I'm not a pedophile; I like pubescent women. We'll dress her as a child. That should help.*

He walked the length of a long and deep closet and drew out a pair of overalls. He fished around in the drawers of a restoration wardrobe to pull out a t-shirt and a pair of bright red socks.

As he carefully cleaned and dressed Nora, Nora sat up briefly, seemed to recognize him, and passed out again.

Good, Michael thought. Now, who is this Andrew? Andrew Frank, director of the CIA? Probably. He clapped his hands and a 15-foot screen emerged with classified data on the CIA director.

Yes, Andrew Frank. Well, Michael thought proudly, *Andrew can't help her, but I can. What do I read for her therapy? Freud again? No, better Breuer, sympathetic to women. Kernberg? Useless except for a few passages on borderline introjects. Bass, best, victim accounts, what the multiples say about themselves, better than those assholes.*

A list of three hundred books appeared on the screen. Michael picked up a handheld; sitting close to Nora, he read. Several hours later, he emerged.

"Send up some food," he ordered through an intercom. "Salmon, walnuts, quinoa, kale, green tea, chocolate ice cream."

Who are the alters? he pondered as he spoon-fed Nora. *Nora, Larissa, the Dead Girl, the Predator, and …*

"Pieces! I am Pieces, Mikey Pieces!" Nora chimed forth, spewing chocolate ice cream on Michael's tailored shirt.

"Who?"

"Pieces, Mikey! And you are Pieces, too!

Michael could not help smiling at the ebullient and confident being in front of him. "How old are you, Pieces? he asked.

"I'm TWOOOOO!"

"You speak very well for a two-year-old," Michael complimented her.

"I spoke in full sentences at the age of three months. In Russian and English. Very early verbal, Mikey Pieces," Pieces replied.

"Why do you call me Mikey Pieces?"

Pieces looked at him sternly. "Don't be disinGENuous, Mikey. You are Pieces like me. You have a smart Mikey Pieces and a very scary small—I mean a very scared small; scary is an infantile trope—a very scary small person inside you, a scary Mickey, little mousey Mickey. My scary is called Lora. Now, are you ready to talk to Nora?"

The serial killer sifted through his feelings. He seemed to hear a small boy begging for help who was pushing away a butcher knife held by his mother. "This is a lot. I don't know," he answered honestly.

"Ready or not." There was Nora, chocolate ice cream dribbling down her face. She looked at Michael with approbation and Michael realized that she found him physically attractive. Confusion became boyish shyness and the serial killer blushed.

"You are not going to hurt me," Nora told him.

"I want to very badly," Michael confessed.

"Not as much as you want to help me. And to know yourself, which I can help you do. Gnosis.

"Gnosis," Michael agreed humbly.

Nora smiled. "How about getting me a towel, Michael? You can't take me seriously with chocolate ice cream all over my face."

"Let's leave it there for now, for safety. I'm not a pedophile. Or a coprophiliac."

"Whatever."

"How do you bounce back from shit like in the Crematorium so fast?" Michael inquired, genuinely curious.

"There is a picture of me next to the word *resilience* in the dictionary, Michael," Nora said proudly. "And God, Michael," she added a little less proudly. "God has always helped me." She turned to an icon of the Blessed Mother above the couch and crossed herself, Orthodox style.

"There's a shitstorm brewing out there, Michael," Nora continued, all business, to Michael's disappointment. "Ouspensky is preparing his troops for a rapture of universal proportions. He's beginning to fear death, realizing his science will only keep him alive as a zombie, as he is keeping my mother alive. He is getting religion. I took his 5th step, his Sex and Love Addict confession, which was quite short; he could only see that he had harmed himself."

Nora took a swallow of kale. "Nice, Mikey!" she smiled through green teeth. "Your cook is better than Ouspensky's!"

"Of course he is," Michael said coldly, resenting the comparison.

"Man up, Michael." A stern and pained face replaced the upbeat Nora/Pieces. "I have been a sexual wind-up toy for hundreds of men, child molesters, sadists, frotteurs, perverts of every stripe. I am a sick woman, disappointed, distrustful, a character out of Dostoevsky. I am at that age when I wonder why I spent so much time chasing men, instead of making money (at my age, an un-face-lifted, un-moisturized, and sugar-binged 54, the only thing that counts is what you have in your wallet and in your brain, with the latter running a poor second to the first.) And what I have in my brain, Michael, is a story so shocking, so extreme, that denizens of Bellevue forensic psychiatry, upon hearing me when I qualify in the SLAA meetings I bring there, whisper "O miss, o miss, I'm sorry that happened to you...."

"However, for the briefest moment, I am sane and Orwell is right, sanity is not statistical. I have broken the codes of the pitiful brainwashing that kept me captive for five decades, and now am free. The horrible foes of my life, the Satanic cult? They are now debile gangsters, octogenarian child molesters, members emeriti of the Union City Klan and Nazi parties. My porn films still circulate, more popular than Betty Page's among a certain clique of high and drunken jet-setters considering reality shows to sustain their various habits: plastic surgery, supplements, young flesh."

"You need help," Michael said. "Therapy. From someone who loves you. Talk therapy."

"And that someone is a psychopathic serial killer. It just may be a lunatic you're looking for. Great." Nora looked at her watch. "You've got one hour."

"Stream of consciousness and free association. Lie down." Michael pointed to the couch. "And unlike Deal, I'll listen."

"Okay, let's try this." Nora inhaled, then exhaled mightily and started. "The Rosen serial covers his victims in 50-dollar bills and then fucks their corpses in the snow. Keeps kills from spring and summer in the cool storage units in the hospital where he works as a stock boy. Rabbit Rosen shares his fantasies with me. "*There is a girl. She works as a waitress at my diner. She is so hot I would fuck her in the snow. I come into the diner and we go to the back. I cover her face and body with fifty-dollar bills and show her my face on the covers of all the sports magazines in the world. And then I leave.*" He walks on his hands for his kills (he is an aging gymnast).

My mind is full of this kind of stuff. My family, my parents: the mind cannot bear a hurt too great to the heart, don't know who said that but that's why I dissociate. Dissociated serial Hans holding a severed head and an axe. Forced victims to take baths in a bathtub full of the severed heads of children. Sweet Hansie, psychopath with at least two alters, one hatchet-wielding and insane. Jim Namrod, a small apelike man, never went anywhere without two shopping bags full of porn...."

"Talk about yourself, not your cases."

"I am a case," Nora retorted. "Okay, I'll try. I remember tracking Bost to the corner of 72nd and Riverside, an apartment across from Ouspensky's digs in New York. Seeing sculptures of three owls on three windowsills, meant to frighten away pigeons, knowing he was in those three rooms. His kill rate went down when we were together. I thought that you and he, incarcerated, could give assistance with serial murder cases like Bundy did. You both helped me when I needed it and were not responsible due to insanity."

Michael scowled. "Nora, you are codependent," he said. "Tell me about yourself, your feelings."

Nora nodded. "I'll try. Well, I believe it is possible that my mother tried to murder my father and that my niece murdered my mother, this before Ouspensky reincarnated her. I believe it is probable that my mother committed infanticide."

"Bost used to say 'we have nothing to fear but gravity and predation.' Also, 'garbage bags are the basis of civilization.' (He puts his victims in garbage bags.) Is very neat and orderly and has beautiful handwriting. Is particle physicist, designs accelerators. Thinks Antonio Gramsci's writings are the philosophical basis of what he calls the group think of modern life."

"Nora ..."

"I'm trying. Well, I love Foucault. He writes about the extraordinary power of mentally ill people, our ability to tolerate amazing things. He describes a madwoman sleeping in the snow. Foucault loved the mad. And I wonder: did my husband Steven have other assets that that my mother and father may have stolen? I think my mother pimped me out to men in my teen years. I have no memory of this; this was probably helped by a lobotomy from Deal. I just remember Mama folding my negligee, packing me and preparing me to go to Cuernavaca. My mother was a love addict; she envied me, the daughter she sold to strange men."

"What about Ouspensky?" Michael inquired, not quite suppressing his jealousy.

"I went back to Ouspensky even after he tortured and killed my brood. I am a stone love addict. Or an undercover cop; sometimes I don't know which. I'm caught in the double bind used by Deal and Mama both: Deal explained my mother to me in our first two years of therapy, he said that that was the key—the double bind: you're good/you're bad. Confusing and harder to reject than uniformly negative messages. He talked about how she used the phone to seduce me 'Pour it out, *dotsinka*, pour it out.'"

"When I first met John Deal, he said my family was the most disturbed constellation he had ever seen. Later (around 2004?) he said that I was his sickest patient."

"My niece and godchild Tara. Protect. I didn't. My grief, rampage smashing the furniture when I thought Tara was incested, blindly walking down trafficked streets in the middle of the road, daring buses to try, try, try motherfuckers to hit me."

"I returned to Deal after this breakdown. He said that Mama called him, saying, 'Nora was never so good as when she was in your care.'"

"Deal also said that he didn't want to help rebuild me after Steven's death. Deal was in on the murder."

Michael nodded. "What would you do to Deal if you could?"

"For refusing to let me talk about a violent and traumatic incident in Switzerland, which resulted in physical and psychological harm to me; for not providing trauma therapy; for overmedicating me; for medicating me when safer and more appropriate therapies were available; for misdiagnosing me; for not being supportive of my 12 step recovery; for not knowing—or pretending not to know—my parents were Holocaust-involved till eight or more years into therapy; for mixing dangerous contraindicated medications; for being verbally and emotionally abusive; for saying sexually inappropriate things; for frequently telling me 'you look like shit' and making comments about my body and weight; for lying; for being a narcissist; for being a fucking nut; for giving me drugs that caused cognitive impairment, that affected my memory and language centers and other parts of my brain, that impaired my ability to learn, especially languages and that changed my affect, denying me emotional richness; for being complicit in attacks against my person; for shaming my sexuality and controlling it with drugs; for talking shit about Tara; for being a sociopath; for not providing me appropriate grief therapy for Tara or Steven; for being part of a cover-up of a murder or murders; for not exploring abuse issues; for being sexist; for attacking me every time I tried to rise above the level of his mediocrity; for telling me who and what I was and what I could be and do; for being a limited, evil man taking up too much space on this planet, I want to sue him for malpractice for every penny he is worth and lock him up for life."

"You go in and out of the realities of your lobotomies and RA programming," Michael commented.

"What do you expect, junior shrink? I go in and out on who you are."

"Good," Michael nodded. "Continue."

"You have 45 minutes left," Nora informed him.

"The cult. Talk about the cult, how they made you feel."

"Paranoid. I couldn't even listen to the Beatles any more. I would listen to the end of the *White Album*, the noises, the 'take this to serve' in the Crowley voice, it sounded like a Black Mass or Satan-worshippers gathering to me. And who is "number nine"? What is the child's voice saying about getting naked? There is the sound of a crying child...."

Nora stood up. She rocked back and forth.

"Mama with a diaper pin, poised at my pupil," she intoned. "Mama telling me never to refuse a man sex. Mama telling me, when I said that people liked me, that they wouldn't if they really knew me. Mama at the end of her life: 'If I had to do it over again, I wouldn't have had children.'"

"In 2016 I saw a dialogue box on my computer that said: *Are there Nazis operating in the United States?* I screamed. "I remember entertaining at an Ouspensky gathering done in Weimar style, *Cabaret* style, all the cult and Nazi organizations met for an orgy. I sang '*Mein Leiber Herr.*'"

"I remember when Mama came down the stairs in the basement one day. Looking for attention, she exclaimed 'I have cancer....' 'Aw, Ma, you don't have cancer,' I said. She lied all the time."

"'I have an instinct for self-preservation. When you are blowing music out the roof and running around wild, people pay attention. If you write 'I was raped, I was incested, I was molested, I was harassed,' people don't pay too much never mind."

"Deal once said that I never refused a gambit. That my responses were rigid. He liked me 'fey,' as though he could construct my personality to suit what he liked."

"He once told me that he loved me, very hesitatingly."

"I thought there was a hit on me in 2016. And recently have thought the same. Would Deal and his SS friends 'do me,' as the good doctor most eloquently might put it himself."

"But these thoughts bring up feelings and I was brought up not to talk, not to trust, and not to feel.

'Feelings,' Mama used to spit in disgust. '*Feeelings*.'"

Michael positioned his glasses, held in his hands, and tried to look thoughtful. "What about Ouspensky?" he asked.

Nora shook her head. "Right now, I just see and feel Ouspensky thrusting his large, uncircumcised cock into my mouth."

Michael turned crimson. "Better tell me something else quickly."

"Will do," Nora said, looking at Michael turning from red to purple. "Leda brought me to the attention of Ouspensky at the age of three, told him I had Naryshkin blood. I often wondered whether I could I have been Ouspensky's blood daughter by Leda, who then hated me for supplanting her both in kin and Nikolai's affections."

"NO … MORE … OUSPENSKY," Michael demanded.

Nora shifted gears quickly. "My parents hated the Soviets (and who could blame them). Leda said that they welcomed the Germans with open arms. She said, 'And that when we found out what the Germans were doing to children, we said no.' As if you could say no in the camps."

"My mother Leda is the cult poisoner. Leda made cyanide from apricot and peach pits. Liked cyanide—it reminded her of Zyklon B during her glory days in Germany and Poland. Mama the grand witch of the RA/Nazi cult, a Ukrainian honored by the Germans for her cruelty in the Dora Frauenblock. She once said quietly to me, 'In America, you must blow your horn; I was taught to be modest.'"

"Leda could be kind, in her way. Once, when I was having difficulty translating a scientific journal, she consoled me by saying, 'Even I could not do that.' Mama pet name for me was *Muchinítsa*, martyr.

"Tara told me Dedushka 'played' with Mama 'under the table.'"

Nora made the *aum* sound and recited, dispassionately.

In the closet

I am in the closet

With Babushka

At home

In Steven's apartment I come out of blackout in his closet with a woman

I am scratching my hand during the Pledge of Allegiance. I am asked by second-grade teacher Miss Kissinger if I have ever been told not to salute the American flag. I thought she meant we were Soviets, but she knew we were Ukrainians.

Tara was murdered.

Tara researching our ancestry, brave child, brave brave brave . . .

"Cold, she was," Deal pronounced. "That should have been caught in med school."

Papa a drunk and child molester an errand boy for the cult but Leda loves him besottedly

Tara and Papa went to Russia. Did he god god goddo to her what he did to me? Deal never discussed Tara's "suicide..."

Nora took hold of herself. "Tara used to say imagine what women could do if they were not thinking constantly about their weight." She whispered, "I will never release you, my child."

Michael nodded vigorously. "You see what a good listener I am," he couldn't help saying. "Keep talking,

Nora, you are healing. I am healing you!"

Nora smiled at her ridiculous shrink. "Deal is unable to understand grief; did not grieve his own wife's death, does not understand my grief for Tara. Nor can you."

"Yes, I can, yes, I can! More free association! More," Michael insisted.

Nora released another *aum* deep from her belly.

Cult members turn on one another like rats. I am in a Russian Orthodox church. There is a ring of votive candles before an icon. I realize that, Guido-Inferno-like, they are the souls of my family. Suddenly, I am lifted off my feet; the flames carry me out of the church. At the entrance, I feel a small but insistent fist in my back. A thin, child-sized hag has attached herself parasitically to me. I turn to face her, and demand: Who is taking care of this child? and the nightmare ends.

Steven repeating over and over again when he first came to my house and met my family, this isn't normal, saying he would get me out of this place, is turned by Leda and his massive indebtedness. I have a baby by Bost—Mama says, don't tell him. Abort, he doesn't want to know.

Steven on the night we met, showing me the Ascent of Man *Bronowski episode about camps and Heisenberg principle, Bronowski on his knees on the film, saying "These people (Nazis) were certain, don't be too sure." They told him how to get me....*

Plato's Retreat in the Ansonia Hotel on W. 74th Street Ouspensky and me in the swimming pool, Dr. Frankenfurter and Janet. Don't dream it, be it....

"Don't talk about Ouspensky!" Michael whined.

Nora was becoming irritated. She looked at Michael's watch. "Okay, I'll talk about Bost. Clinical. Emotionless except for self-pity. Reaction to mother's death unemotional, detached. Father racist and paranoid. Grew up in Bund country. Bost racist; believes blacks and women 'get all the grants.' Dishonest. Sense of entitlement. Difficulties with empathy. Into superiority."

"In 2016, harassed and convinced that there was a hit on me; feeling, as I had in the past, that I was unable to even take care of my dog. I met Bost at the *International Book Store* in the West Village, first reaction: thought he seemed goofy and unfocused. At Cedar Tavern after my reading, he told me of his suicide attempt playing Russian roulette and I felt my rib go out to him, Eve to Adam; fell into oceanic, trance-like love. Possibly the first person whose physical well-being was as important as Tara's to me. Married. I ignored the most basic of rules—avoid married men. He was handsome and somehow humbler then."

"Everybody plays the fool, sometime. There's no exception to the rule, the song goes. Love bonkers all."

"Bost firmly believed he was the most intelligent person in the world. Deal used to laugh at how I fed into that belief."

"Bost drunk, high, raving that he knew Navy Seals. Enjoyed action movies. Blowing his cover with me every day, but I didn't pick up on it."

Ne soprotivlenie zlu zlom.

"If Ouspensky is a narcissist then am I his narcissistic rival? First idealized, then a threat to the homosexual relationship with father, relationship with mother? Ouspensky a classical narcissist, idealizes me, then devalues me when he has me, then falls into depression when I leave and cut off his narcissistic supply, only wants me, idealizes me again from a distance. Ouspensky keeps lists of everyone he fucked, claims a fuckline back the Peter the Great."

"Ouspensky said 'men are about fucking and fighting and women are about making babies.' Crude betimes, dear Ousp."

"I befriended John Lennon, learned that he was framed. He played me a lost Beatle song:

"Your mother's gone. / Did you try? / Your mother's gone. / Did she fly?"

I also dated Stephen Falcon, who at age five debunked M-theory with a new multiverse equation and at the age of thirteen invented a rocket fuel that could power an interstellar craft. Ouspensky is missing an element and, dear Michael, the element he needs to create it? The Birds' bodies contain it. Falcon has explained the workings of various particle accelerators to me and has told me how to disarm them. Deformed body, albino, unable to sit without support. This is the smartest man in the world, and I have such a crush on him!"

NORA: There. That was cathartic. Thank you for listening to my animadversions.

MICHAEL: Don't you want my feedback?

NORA: Nah, not really, serial. Okay, Michael, your turn. Are you powerless over rape and murder and skinning your victims alive and has your life become unmanageable?

MICHAEL: (LOOKING AROUND HIS APARTMENT) I wouldn't say unmanageable.

NORA: You're not ready.

MICHAEL: You won't abreact me until I admit this?

NORA: Nope.
MICHAEL: Damn, this shit is hard. (THE MEDIOCRITY EMERGES FOR A SECOND, SCREAMS.)
NORA: (PRESSING) You believe God can help you?
MICHAEL: I know you do. Is that enough?
NORA: Okay, let's back up. Are you willing to believe there is a Power greater than you?
MICHAEL: Than me? Haven't met him yet.
NORA: You are not ready.
MICHAEL: This 12-step stuff is the real cult.

"Don't get touchy," Nora grinned. "Okay, so now, Ouspensky has sought out the Dalai Lama. The spiritual leader has told him not to fear death, that death is actually the most beautiful and enjoyable event in human life, a union with God and the cosmos in the final moments in the human form. Ouspensky can't resist a high. He has nominally repented of his sexual sins (he had a relapse with me, he can't resist my masochism vis-à-vis him) and wants the whole universe to share in this transcendent moment with him as an amends for what he knows somewhere in his soul was a horrible life; he believes himself the only one grand enough to do it. This is why he is so set on destroying the universe; being Ouspensky, he thinks his end justifies his means, which is why he rapes, murders, and mayhems to achieve it. This makes him almost unstoppable."

"Yes, yes, I can stop him, no sweat," Michael interrupted. "I'd like you to see the Doll House now," he added impulsively. *Think of me, not your damn Genya.*

"Are you turning yourself in or showing off?"

"Both. If I can turn myself into you. I'll save the

universe first, but you have to come look at my art, or no deal."

Nora rose and wiped the chocolate off her face with her shirt. "Today I will judge nothing that occurs," she said under her breath. "Let's get this over with."

Michael led her to a bank of older wooden elevators, ornately carved. They rode down to the basement—*Of course, like Ouspensky's cave,* Nora thought. The Doll House had to be in the basement, a thing of deep and sick subconscious.

Michael almost writhed in excitement as the elevator door opened.

On the floor, in glass cages with painted settings as with big game at the Museum of Natural History, were Jackie U in a pastel pillbox hat, a muscular Pam Grier as Foxy Brown, Lady Gaga in her meat dress, and Kim Kardashian's rounded ass next to Caitlin Jenner. To the left was a row of women who looked like Nora, dressed in gym clothes, police uniforms, and evening gowns, and to the right, the Rockettes dressed for the annual Radio City Christmas show. It was hard for Nora to believe the figures were not alive, even after feeling their stillness for long minutes. The women were beautiful and vibrant, a triumph over death.

Michael pointed to the figure of a young Paris Hilton, holding a preternaturally life-like chihuahua and a small toy drum. "Susie," Michael began explaining haltingly to Nora, "You see, I do … I did …" He could not continue.

Nora stared, glared, frozen for long moments, then hit him with all her might. They both vomited.

"This is just the anteroom," Michael explained, still

wheezing from Nora's belly blow. "There are many more floors...."

Nora stood upright. She looked at Michael with hatred.

"I can't handle this. Larissa," she pleaded. "Please take over.

Certainly, my dear, Larissa answered. Her five-foot-three frame seemed to tower over Michael.

I am Larissa Ekaterina Anastasia Nikolayevna Romanova, tsaritsa of all the Russias. Kneel, slave, she commanded him.

"Her name was Susie," Michael sobbed as he knelt.

"They all had names. What is your real name?"

"Gus. August. August Smith," Michael sputtered.

"Hold yourself together while I speak to you. You are sorry for this, Gus?"

"Very sorry. I feel guilty."

"A little guilty, but more proud of your genius still, yes?"

"Yes."

"You will not do this abomination again."

"I might."

"You will decide now to turn your will and life over to the care of God, and will not perp again."

"I so decide."

"Amends must be made. Help Nora save the planet, help me remove that *puto* Ouspensky and that other *puto* in Russia, give full disclosure to the authorities and the families. Do you agree?"

"I agree."

"We will go with you to the lethal injection. That we

promise. We will be there with you at your end."

"Thank you. But if I save the world ..."

"It's not equivalent. You know that. The one doesn't erase the other. Susie was a world unto herself. "

Michael and Gus sobbed.

"Calm yourself and resign yourself," Larissa said, making the sign of the Orthodox cross above him. "You are a dead man walking."

"I am so resigned."

"You are not, but we will discuss this further as your abreaction continues. Let us leave this place."

Larissa led Nora and a conflicted Gus back to his spacious living room. "Can you take it from here?" she asked Nora.

"I think so."

As Nora reemerged, so did confident, self-loving Michael.

"Nora," he asked her as eagerly as a teenager. "Do you think I am handsome? Do you think I am sexy?"

"Yes, and your voice is golden. That's how you lured all those girls, teenagers most of them, to their death."

"But you are 54. I won't kill you."

"Can I talk to Gus, please?"

"No," Michael objected vehemently. "I want you to be attracted to me, Michael. I'm the brilliant one, the one who's gonna save the planet."

Nora vomited again, aiming deliberately for the white cashmere couch. "All right," she said, wiping her mouth. "Let's get the fuck to work. First of all, Ouspensky never met the Dalai Lama; I just was seeing how much assholic stupid counterintel you would swallow; that's

Ouspensky's feed. Ouspensky wants to rule the world and the particle accelerators are the main hardware in his arsenal. He holds, or thinks he holds, CERN....

Suddenly, a series of urgent caws reverberated deafeningly in the cavernous room, shaking the Rothkos and the icons.

"Gotta go, Mikey." Nora gulped down the remaining salmon. "I'm taking your copter."

"I'm going, too," a four-year old voice insisted.

Nora smiled. "Okay, Mickey-Pieces," she said to a confused Michael. "Let's go save the world."

***

Lesbian Audrey Uhuru stared at Bost with loathing, unmoved by his hypermasculine movie star looks. "Anybody ever tell you you look like a Ken doll, Bost?" she sneered. "Bet the anatomical details match. We always thought you used a dildo." She reached for her gun and her cuffs. "You have the right to remain silent," she began.

Andrew shamefacedly shook his head "no."

Audrey glared at her boss. "You are kidding me," she said, each word choked with rage, knowing full well that the CIA chief was not. She moved to cuff Bost.

"Stand down, Uhuru," Andrew ordered.

Bost smiled a supercilious and triumphant smile. "They let me have my fun as long as I'm useful," he told Audrey. "And I am quite useful, now more than ever," he continued as Audrey cuffed him. In an instant, Bost had freed himself from the cuffs. Audrey moved to tackle him.

"Stand down, Audrey," Andrew said gently. "I will explain later."

Bost handed Audrey's pick-proof cuffs back to the now composed agent, who promised herself that she would have Andrew's job in a year.

Shevchenko addressed Bost, trying to mask the repugnance she felt for him. "You are the author of 'Multiverse 17' and the reply to the Higgs boson paper I published in 2011," she stated.

Bost's left eyebrow raised. "I suppose it was obvious, but how did you know?"

The laureate's attempt at civility strained her. "From the author's contempt for female physicists, and your signature, Niels Bost, which is tattooed on your wrist. The paper bore a similar signature, your pseudonym Niels Bore, which ... well ..." The laureate could not continue. "We shall discuss these ideas later; now, I have to talk to the Birds." She left the lab with visible relief.

"We will join you in a minute." Andrew turned to Audrey. "Perhaps you would like to join Professor Shevchenko?"

"Yes," Audrey replied, "I would very much like to join Professor Shevchenko. But somebody has to take notes at this meeting, right, boys?" She dug her heels in and leaned back in her chair.

"I really think ..." Bensinck began; Andrew nodded. But one look at the lesbian's face, and the men backed down.

Bost smiled at the black female operative, who smiled back, knowing full well he was planning her rape. "Ken doll," she laughed sotto voce.

"Audrey!" Andrew commanded. "Let's do this," he ordered the others.

Bost began. "Ouspensky holds, or thinks he holds, the following accelerators: BEPC I, CESR, DAFNE (LNF), KEK-B, LHC (CERN), RHIC (BNL), SLC (SLAC), TESLA (DESY), VEPP-3, VEPP-4M, VEPP-2000 (BINP).

"That's all the colliders in the world!" Andrew exclaimed.

"Almost," Bensinck interjected. "I have constructed three privately, in Italy, Switzerland, and Germany. The German Hadron collider is in Nordhausen, built on the ruins of a primitive but functioning frame model constructed in 1944."

"Impossible!" Bost sneered.

"My modern-day colliders or the Nordhausen one?" Bensinck inquired politely.

"Either." Bost's pinky, on which there was a death's head ring, twitched almost unperceptively. "I would have known."

Bensinck smiled delicately. "Perhaps less recreation and more attention to intel?" he suggested to the glowering Bost.

"The science in 1944 …" Bost began.

"Truly could not have built it. Without extraterrestrial help. As Dr. Shevchenko is learning now, even as we speak." Bensinck turned up the volume on a nearby speaker. Shevchenko was translating the Birds simultaneously now, about their first pilgrimage to Nordhausen, and their work with Werner von Braun and his translator, Leda Alexenko Volkhonsky, to build the V-2 rockets and the world's first particle accelerator, a doomsday weapon.

"So, the Birds are Nazis?" Andrew asked, his

frustration fully evident.

"Nazi slaves. Technical first circle experts. They escaped to seek out Nora, whose brain waves they picked up somewhere near Aldebaran. Based on her brain structure, they believe she is the only non-Nazi in the universe, and have come to seek her help. They also would like to kill Nora's mother, Leda."

"Not Nora's mother," said Shevchenko from above. "Leda Alexenko was a surrogate," the Birds were telling Shevchenko, who now was cawing fluently. "The egg was of the Tsarina Alexandra, wife of Nicholas II, who was as limited and unpopular as Leda. The egg was stored and planted in the healthy young Ukrainian collaborator as an immigrant in Brooklyn."

"Nora used to call me Rasputin in her love letters to me," Boast mused affectionately. "So, in vitro technology?"

Shevchenko spoke clearly and quickly, cawing *yes* periodically at her pterodactylane interlocutors to verify the quickening flow of information. "Also, from the Birds: Alexandra was German, and that race seemed the best for spreading Nazism in the terrestrial twentieth century. The Birds' masters are banking on twenty-first-century America led by The Howard as presidential figurehead for Nazism here on in."

Bensinck interrupted. "Nora's, that is, Larissa Nikolayevna's claim to the Russian throne?"

"Larissa, Nora's alter, is Russian to the core, and all Russians always hated Nazis until this Stalin-nostalgia manifested itself in the current ruler. And Nora was born in Brooklyn, and there has never been a real Nazi from Brooklyn, at least not a native. And there is the issue of Nora's brain, which suggests some alien spermatozoa might have entered our beloved friend's genomic mix."

"And Ouspensky doesn't really want to give the universe the cosmic experience of death, right?" Audrey asked. "That's a love-addict fantasy he planted in Nora's brain. He wants to hold the world hostage with a reverse Big Bang until he places a lobotomized, robotized Nora on the throne of Russia with himself as regent consort."

"Yes, that is the plan, Audrey," Bensinck concurred. "Nora's discernment is notoriously poor around Ouspensky. Yes, he wants the throne of his mother Russia as it was at the height of its empire, from Finland to Turkey to Mongolia, a throne he believes was denied him by a trick of fate—his forbears should have ruled, by his estimation, from the time of Catherine. With The Howard as a close ally in the United States, he plans a swift annexation of China and India. Ussasis will control the European Union. Being utter racists and 100 years behind geopolitically, the triad believe it will be easy setting up puppet states throughout Africa and South America."

Audrey nodded. "And these will all be Nazi states?"

"Negative." Andrew aimed his handheld at Bensinck's screen, and an image of the dark-maned, blue-eyed Ouspensky appeared, his handsome features enhanced by imperceptible makeup and an elegantly wild coiffure. "Ouspensky doesn't care what kind of states he rules over, as long as he is the boss and everyone else suffers. He's a sadist: Nazism, deep-south plantation slavery, bricks without straw pyramids—it doesn't matter to him a bit, as long as people are hurting." Andrew paused and smiled ruefully. "Well, not exactly; he does have preferences. He especially likes to see children, innocents, kind people suffer. He likes to see if he can corrupt and dehumanize them, pervert them, make them as evil as he is. This gives him joy and tremendous sexual satisfaction. Nora's good and cheerful nature has presented an especially fun, if frustrating, challenge to him. He tortures her, but she never seems to turn."

Bost agreed. "She never does," he said kindly. The rest stared at him and his out-of-character affect.

Bost shrugged. "She's a nice person ..." he began.

But caws sounding like screams flooded the yacht's public address speakers and overrode the thought. Shevchenko's voice could be heard above the Bird's terrified cries. "Hey, CIA, Bensinck, you had better get up here," the diminutive laureate was shouting at the top of her lungs. The men and Audrey ran, not knowing what to expect.

***

Nora and August Smith, AKA Michael and Mikey-Pieces, emerged from an industrial elevator onto the Tudor City building helipad. The Birds were frozen above the East River. Only their voices could be heard; their terror and anguish required no translation. Hovering near them was a carrier for a communications satellite, emblazoned with swastikas.

Nora's phone rang. On the screen was her father, looking well for a nonagenarian.

"Greetings, daughter," Nikolai Volkhonsky said, his right arm in a Heil salute, as Nora's phone revealed a relaxed handsome older man on the bridge of a spacecraft that looked like a spacious and comfortable Spacelab. "As usual, I find you in the middle of all kinds of shit."

"Hello, Papa," Nora answered. "Great to see you, too. You seem to have kept up with your old friends, or masters, I should say, since you are and always will be a Slav *untermensch* to them."

Nikolai smiled. "I will soon have the opportunity to spank you for your uppity talk, my dear whore of a daughter."

"So, there are Nazis in outer space. Ho-hum," Michael chimed in.

"Is this your current mate, Nora?" Nikolai's tone tempered and sweetened as a petite and leathery-skinned alien whispered in his ear.

"Yes!" Michael screamed as Andrew's voice yelling "No!" came on over Nora's phone, to Nora's delight and Michael's jealous rage.

"Alien craft, you are in Earth airspace. Identify yourself or be fired upon," Andrew said authoritatively. From his tone, Nora could tell he was being fed instructions, maybe from the Pentagon or higher.

"I am Nikolai Fyodorovich Volkhonsky, father of the *kurva* Nora Nikolayevna Volkhonsky, captain of our race's flagship, the S.S. *Werner von Braun*, and commander of the Braunulan fleet, some ten vessels of which are now approaching your magnetosphere. The satellite you see is armed with fusion devices beyond your science."

"The master race of Braunulus demands the immediate disarmament of all Earth particle accelerators or Earth will be destroyed by us. You have 48 hours."

"Not your master race, Daddy-o, you *untermensch schwein*," Nora chimed in sweetly.

"Nora Volkhonsky, you are broadcasting internationally. Stand down," Andrew ordered.

"*OOOOONTERmensch*," Nora cried again, and then silenced herself as one of the Birds shrieked and fell into the East River.

Nora's phone lit up with calls from FBI, CIA, NATO, and POTUS. She took Shevchenko's. "Nora, this is me, Aura," Shevchenko said urgently. "Listen, this is what the Birds told me. The Braunulans head a coalition of Nazi-inspired planet states with Valkyrie-like leaders. Like our Nazis, they are into physical fitness and *gemutlichkeit* and slavery and extermination of smart people and have come to destroy Earth if Ouspensky's particle accelerators armed to Big Bang the cosmos out of existence are not disarmed in 48 hours. They want you as a hostage."

"No!" Michael and Andrew said simultaneously.

"Your father corrects this. Guests, not hostages. You and your handsome mate."

"Me!" Michael cried. "They mean me! Let's go, babe, I'll watch your back."

"No!" Andrew screamed through the phone as the satellite landed on Michael's helipad and Nora and the Jersey Skinner climbed up the thin stairs into the pulsing and arachnid-like red-and-black craft.

***

Ouspensky slapped his manicurist hard. "Cunt!" he squealed. "Be more careful!" His eye lazily wandered over to the gigantic screen on the opposite wall: YouSuck TV.

Ouspensky's time-warp escape hatch is revealed; he and his allies and minions can survive the reverse Big Bang in multiverse 17. In secret, he has struck a deal with the Nazis, promising to join their Federation and offering extremely promising trade incentives and slave labor if they let him rule the Earth. Nora's father invites Nora and Michael, whom he presumes to be her mate, to asylum on a Nazi coalition planet, hoping to breed his daughter for her unusual brain, and then turn her over to slow and agonizing torture.

"No!" Ouspensky shouted. "Rewrite! Time-play rewrite! The Nora cunt establishes me as Russian regent first."

"We know that," Nikolai Volkhonsky signaled back. "Just humor us."

Nikolai shows Nora and Michael holograms of clean and verdant plains, unpolluted, rich with animal species that are larger than Earth's, since their habitats have not been destroyed and can support their great size. Nora looks at a herd of cattle the size of giant wildebeests grazing peacefully beneath two yellow suns. The untermenschen *slaves are green aliens who disappear into the background. Only their large eyes can be seen; they look terrified and thin as they herd the great beasts.*

"Okay," Ouspensky said into a mike. "After a brief commercial break for *Mein Kampf* family camping, we will come back with a flashback: The origins of the beloved ruler of Earth, Genya the Great!"

We see Ouspensky as a clever and habile infant in his nursery and then on the battlefield, watching his SS father in action, torturing, raping, mutilating, maiming, with a predilection for prepubescent girls.

"And, of course, *my* bio," Nikolai Volkhonsky interrupted.

Ouspensky nodded assent peevishly. "After a brief commercial break for *Mein Kampf*, family camphor for the chest, we return to Nora's father," he said.

We see Nikolai in his Earth life as a trainer of Ukrainian kapos in the WWII extermination camps and a serial killer in Russia, Germany, the United States, and parts of Canada. He kills prostitutes with a Revlon nail clipper file. The Green River Killer emulates him.

"Ho hum," Ouspensky yawned. "It should really all be about me, but put this in for continuity. 'If the Braunulans are escaped Nazis, how can they affect events before

World War II?' Sad to think that anyone bright enough to ask that question must be exterminated as a threat. Maybe we can play with them first, as with that slut Nora … no, too dangerous. The Braunulans are right: she's a walking-talking shitstorm. Here goes the explanation, which might be the truth; who gives a fuck, really?"

The Braunulans have a temporal device that can return people to the past. So far, they can't alter the past, but they can occasionally drop technologies in before their time in small ways that don't affect history. They are working on a particle-wave dome based on Heisenberg's uncertainty principle, based on the idea that memory, like observation, can alter elapsed space-time, which exists as an elastic wave; acoustic, space-time thus requires a medium, but is also radiant and corpuscular and mediumless, as in states of electromagnetic radiation. This is the ultimate GUT theory, unifying sound and quantum gravity.

***

The dome before Michael and Nora was in the shape of a half-dead, half-alive cat; their alien guide explained that the Braunulans called it "the *Schrödinger*." This flying laboratory was surrounded by the firepower of ten ships, including the *S.S. von Braun*. Young Nazi scientists with beards and long hair were playing with puzzles, scribbling equations on whiteboards, and reading Shevchenko's work on handheld devices. In the background, a metal band was chanting the current Braunulan hit, "Heil Hamsun:"

Got a medal from Hitler

I wear it on my heart
Got a medal from Hitler
I got it for my art....

Nora thought of the befuddled 80-year-old Knut Hamsun, ignored by Ibsen when he applied for help there as a young artist, accepting Hitler's award. "Nazi rock," she explained to Michael. Michael, fascinated by the dome, wandered off to examine its geodesic lines.

Nora turned her attention to YouSuck on the wall. A loop of a film of Ouspensky as a young scientist, called *The First Creator*, showed him applying the Poisson Distribution to the number of decays in radioactive argon. And to his fan mail.

"You can see me, can't you?" she told the screen.

Ouspensky stretched and flipped the YouSuck channels. "Do this next," he commanded lazily. The screen obediently tracked Nora on the Braunulan spacecraft, commanding her alien guide to depart.

Nora took a closer look at Braunulan physicists' equations, which she recognized as Shevchenko's work.

"Bost's work, cunt," Ouspensky commented as the manicurist licked his nails.

Nora saw, under Ouspensky's rule, that Bost's plagiarism would erase Shevchenko's accomplishments. Nora addressed the video camera. "You tiny wick, I know what you are doing here and it won't work. Truth is truth and truth will out."

From an adjacent screen Nora's father sighed. "Dear ignorant cunt of a daughter, if you are that; you certainly have not inherited my good looks. Have you not heard of the Great Goebbels and 'If the lie is big enough'? If your regent and husband-to-be, dear Tsaritsa, does not erase the little whore Shevchenko, along with Hypatia, Ada Lovelace, Curie, Chien, Carson, and the rest of the female scientists from memory, we, the Braunulans, most certainly will."

"Get spanked, Dad. I'm busy."

Nikolai Volkhonsky grinned. "Yes, you will be. We are going to torture you with new techniques, unimaginably painful and debasing. We will break you this time, and you will be our slave.

"Michael?" Nora asked nervously. Nora turned to look; where had he gone?

"No help there. No help anywhere." A projection flashed in a widening rotating circle on the spacecraft wall. On YouSuck, Nora saw a guide taking Michael to the interior of the *Schrödinger* dome to meet the most prominent Braunulan physicist-philosopher, Wordlock, whom Michael peppered with questions. Wordlock seemed to appreciate Michael's boldness and intelligence, telling Michael that he loved the predator in him.

"Now we will restore you to your true genius," Wordlock exclaimed.

"It's a trap!" the YouSuck mascot, The Howard in leather pants, cried out on the screen.

"Of course it is!" Ouspensky shook his head in disgust. "Intelligent allies are so hard to find," he complained, and then remembered himself. "Present Braunulan company excepted," he added reluctantly. "Continue."

"Nora!" Michael yelled, but a dozen Braunulans overpowered him and stretched him out on an ominous rack in a corner of the flying lab.

"Now we will begin mind programming to return you

to your full serial-killer self, without the useless memories and emotions caused by these sissy abreactions," Wordlock declared. "We will restore the great hunter in you, admired throughout the known universe."

Remembering past abreactions, Michael almost welcomed this treatment. It had been easier to be a cold and calculating killing machine. A buzz began and suddenly sememes and notes and sensations of heat and itching and pleasure overwhelmed him, while a voice like Johnny Depp's kept repeating, "Am I going too fast for you?"

Ouspensky slipped into a black-and-red nightie. "Do this next."

Michael regresses, or un-regresses, and becomes a danger to Nora again. Nora is too old to breed using even the most advanced interstellar ovarian technologies and her father discards her. Michael looks forward to her torture.

"Now we are getting to the good part!" Ouspensky cried, rubbing lotion on his face and feet and settling in for a good watch.

Nora is taken to the Braunulan torture ship. Nora knows the Braunulans can torture her to unimaginable extremes, that she will beg and lose all dignity; even Larissa will not withstand it. Willing herself to die will not help; they will wake her, bring her back, and create new, more hideous tortures. She will no longer be human, but their slave, to do their bidding, whatever it may be.

The only thing that separates us from the Nazis is meaning. Victor Frankl, help me, Nora prayed.

They will torture me, give me hope, just to smash it again. It is more devastating if you hope. An attendant will be kind to me for a few moments, I will believe that there is kindness, help in the world; torture is more effective that way, it is Deal's double bind, and it works. Dear God, help me, truly let them kill me, it will be a mercy, but they have no mercy, they are merciless, and I will never die, I will suffer in Deal's hell for eternity, or until I break and become Ouspensky's slave. What did I do to deserve this, God?

Deal was in charge of the Braunulan torture team.

"I am bringing the clangs back," Deal told Ouspensky.

Ouspensky yawned loudly. "And that worked not at all. You really are a moron, Deal."

"Wait, Genya, hear me out!" Deal cried.

Ouspensky's eyes widened and nostrils flared with rage. "Dr. Ouspensky to you, you quack," he snapped. "I would punish your impertinence if you were worth the trouble. Well, what next?"

"I am sending subliminal messages that she will be abandoned by everyone. First, they will say they are coming to rescue her, but then, when the PET scans attached to her lobes flash sites associated with Michael or Andrew or Audrey, Nora will hear "This is the end, babe. No one likes troublemaking little bitches like you" in their voices. A few positive and hopeful messages, then that and only that."

Ouspensky looked at his royally purple nails. "And"?

"Nora is guarded by Nazgûl-like aliens holding tongs

and scalpels who say, 'We will delicately, so sweetly, eat your cunt ...'"

"Real Nazgûl, or is this an implanted idea?" Ouspensky asked, his interest piqued slightly.

"Real Nazgûl aliens, but they are more frightening and more forbidding due to the subliminal messages. They have this acute predatory interest in her that almost seems friendly. The Nazgûls do love their food. They will double-bind her and slowly and methodically slice up her labia and clitoris."

"Here's a good one, Genya—I mean, Dr. Ouspensky," Deal continued. "I'm having her confabulate that she is a victim of Hatchet Hansie, one of her serial cases who was a hypnotist. He is bathing her in the severed heads of children whom he says she killed. He tries to make her kill children, she won't. Then he hypnotizes her and she thinks she has. The children look like her own, the breeder rats. It's a heavy recall cue to the Chalet, which will be agonizing to her."

Happy, Deal was building up steam. "Then I do flashbacks to our therapy and make her believe she causes the serials to kill, that she is a serial, that she is a Nazi. It's all good." Deal paused as if to admire his handwork. "This next is especially nice. I stimulate this network to create the feeling of a crashing emotional bottom, but also the sense of help; then I totally destroy all hope of it. Here's her early writing it's based on:

... two days on sugar, interrupted only by comatose sleep, I experienced the eunoia again in a psychotic break. The police, who protectively surround me in neighboring apartments, were monitoring my keyboard, waiting for me to type evidence against my Nazi-sympathizer parents,

against the rapist Bost, to provide them with the details and leads they needed to break these cases. Periodically, as what I type becomes too painful for the words which contain them, they play music from their stations on my apartment floor, sending these messages of hope and encouragement, reminders that I am loved and cared for and protected, and that there was good and joy in the world.

I see a tall man with a floppy hat and long curly hair and a kind craggy face on the street; I smile at him and he seems happy to see me....

Ouspensky grunted with rage. "I have a special place in Hell for the fucking two-faced sneak Batty Bensinck. Fool me; steal my kids, dare he?" He turned to Deal. "You had better come up with a truly exquisite torture for that traitor."

Deal pointed at the lab screen and wiggled with joy. In Nora's simulated mind, the Baron Batty Bensinck was sneering, saying to Nora, "Go fuck yourself, you whore bitch."

Next was Andrew, running. To save...?

"Not you, you stupid fucked-up cunt. Who would want a fucked-up whore like you?"

Audrey?

"There are limits, Nora. You passed yours a long time ago."

Aura?

"We have to save the world and you keep fucking everything up. You can't be allowed to do that. Goodbye."

Bost?

"You are a loser, Nora. Everyone and everything is better off without you."

Jesus and Mary?

"This is a big universe and we have a lot of work to do. Take care, Nora."

Larissa?

"There is no Larissa. You are not a queen, just a dirty, useless, troublemaking cunt."

Ouspensky watched Deal dance for joy as the real Nora was dragged into lab by orcs and alien *kapo* collaborators. Nora shook off the henchmen, removed mace from her boot and sprayed them all.

"I thought she didn't fight back anymore!!!" Ouspensky shrieked.

Nora faced the YouSuck cameras. "Genya, dear," she said smiling," I would like to affirm that what other people think of me is none of my business, that I love and accept myself, Nora Volkhonsky, exactly as I am, and that I am worthy and deserving of love, and that I don't need the approval of others. Thank you, Louise Hay! Catch you later, Genya; *à bientôt*."

Ouspensky frothed at the mouth. "How can she be doing this! Stop her!"

"Excuse me, Genya. Mind-forged manacles: What do we do about mind-forged manacles? We discard them." Nora spoke one-by-one to the four YouSuck cameras in the torture chamber. "You have not tied me down or immobilized me in any way, mentally or even physically, creeps." To the surprise of Ouspensky and the Braunulan high command, she walked out of the lab.

"What about the Nazgûl?" screamed Ouspensky.

Nora shook her head. "What about them?" A Nazgûl approached Nora and she punched him. The rest ran away.

Ouspensky stormed out of his quarters and ran to the lab and began slapping and pinching Deal.

"Wait, wait, Dr. Ouspensky, please," Deal squealed. "I am feeding her a substance like a basic neurotransmitter or neurotransmitter agonist."

Nora paused before a YouSuck monitor. "How are they drugging me?" she asked, curious.

"Through titrated modulation of nocioception," Deal answered.

"Why are you talking to her, you idiot!" Ouspensky howled.

"I thought you asked me that," Deal whimpered. "Please don't hit me again."

"Substance P?" Nora asked?

"Yes, substance P," Deal answered robotically.

Ouspensky turned as purple as his nails."WHY ARE YOU TELLING HER THIS, YOU IDIOT!?!"

"Well, she asked and I keep thinking you are asking," Deal whined.

"I'm a regular ventriloquist," Nora boasted and then opened her phone and read: *Nociception (also nocioception or nociperception) is the encoding and processing of harmful stimuli in the nervous system, and, therefore, the ability of a body to sense potential harm. Substance P is an important element in pain perception. The sensory function of substance P is thought to be related to the transmission of pain information into the* central nervous system. *Substance P coexists with the* excitatory neurotransmitter glutamate *in primary afferents that respond to painful stimulation.*

"The potential for analgesics through substance P titration. Even fucking Deal gets that," Nora muttered.

"And torture." She remembered that pepper sauces with the highest levels of capsaicin had been shown to reduce the levels of substance P. "Thus, capsaicin is clinically used as an analgesic. Substance P has been known to stimulate cell growth, including neurons, in culture. "Okay, buy some Scorned Woman hot sauce and figure out if the P substance they are flooding me with has stimulated neurogenesis. They are making me smarter!"

Nora laughed. "Now where's the helm and communication system? Here. Okay, Earth and Braunulans: I'm at the helm of the *Schrödinger* and have access to and know how to use the Braunulan fusion devices. Okay, you guys?"

"Listen to me: There are a hundred brain scans from friend and foe on me 24-seven, Earth and interstellar. I don't need to let everybody know what I'm thinking, and must tell you now that I have, shall we say, misrepresented myself. I'm not even a multiple—but it's great camouflage. That dick Ouspensky thinks I'm in love with him. Do you realize the fucking tactical advantage that gives me? He's listening to this right now and the jerk cannot, will not believe what he is hearing, he is that vain. So, all of you please shut up and just do what I tell you to do from now on. I am the only one here coding with a full set of instructions."

"Nora, are you all right?" Andrew's voice on her phone sounded concerned.

"Yes, and I am 100 percent capable to take command of this op, which I am doing NOW!" Nora said. "Audrey, Aura."

"Yes, Nora," the FBI agent and Shevchenko said.

"You handle the Braunulans and the Birds."

"Will do," the women replied.

"Bensinck?"

"Yes, madam?" the Baron asked.

"Shut down the particle accelerators. And thank you."

"Yes, Madam."

"Excuse me." It was the almost humble voice of Niels Bost. "But you don't know …"

"That they have a sniper called Zero after me, and that she is the best in the business…."

"Except for me," Bost interrupted.

"You will be my bodyguard."

"Michael?"

"Yes, Nora?"

"Where are you? Think hard so I can hear you."

"The Braunulans are holding me prisoner. They say I am alone and that you hate me and …"

"So?"

"What do you mean?"

"You have the opportunity to make some amends now by saving the planet. I will now start your full abreaction. CIA physicians will finish. You will not kill yourself but live to make amends to the victims' families and this planet. Do you agree? Are you ready?"

"Yes."

"Then bust yourself out of there and meet me on the bridge."

"What? Wait, I can! But I'll skin you …"

"No, you fucking won't. Photographer. Mikey Pieces."

"Oh shit. Oh yeah. Oh shit, it's all coming to me—Hannah, Irene, Jodie, Kathleen—I killed them alphabetically…."

"Come to the bridge and we'll continue. Overpower your guard and escape."

"Dead. Coming now. Commander Volkhonsky!"

"Andrew?"

"This is Frank. Volkhonsky, this is highly unorthodox. I am chain of command here."

"Call me Nora; my idiot father might get confused. This is an unorthodox situation, Andrew. I'm going after Ouspensky. Just deal with everything else that comes up and please ask me to go ice skating again some time, okay?"

A full and happy silence followed. "I think I'm getting the hang of this telepathy stuff," Andrew said, a grin in his voice.

Nora couldn't help but pause and grin herself. She shook the happy trance off.

"OKAY, GENYAAAAAAAAAAAAAAAAA!" Nora screamed, gunning the controls on the Braunulan torture ship. "Here we come!"

***

As he made his escape, Michael turned and faced the YouSuck cameras mounted along the walls of the *Schrödinger* dome. "Hey, Nick!" he yelled. "Hey, Ouspensky, you old fart! Do THIS!"

En route to Nora, Michael frees a roomful of hyperlibidinal bipolar women, Nikolai Volkhonsky's harem on the great warship. They are manic and horny, and throng him, and it is all he can do to get away from them. He grins, though. On the bridge of the S.S. Werner von Braun, *Nikolai Volkhonsky scowls.*

"Hey, can anybody play?" yelled Nora. "DO THIS!!! Take me home, space-time!"

Ignoring even the messages from POTUS, Nora landed a small spacecraft in Central Park, and returned to her Upper West Side apartment, dismissing the body guards sent by Andrew.

"Gotta get Joyce," she said, punching in her superhousekeepers's number. In three hours, the disaster-area apartment was sparkling, and she was playing computer chess with Bost, who was in the adjoining apartment with a modified AK-338 on his knees.

Bost overturned his king. "How?"

"Bostie, you always offer that gambit; it's your way of saying, here, I can give you materiel and still win with one hand behind my back. I simply refused the gambit. Most judges will call a stalemate at this point, but you know that, in 14 moves, I will win.

"But you are not logical."

"Who told you that?"

***

"THIS HAPPENS NEXT," Ouspensky howled.

Michael and Nora are captured again. This time it looks grim and Michael asks Nora to abreact him as his dying wish. The Braunulans have given the couple wine as they wait for their execution.

SCENE: MICHAEL'S ABREACTION

NORA: Are you willing to live according to spiritual principles, Michael?

MICHAEL: (DRUNK OFF HIS ASS ON BRAUNULAN WINE) You mean I sloudn't lie sleet or cheal? What if good guys really finish last, Nora? Look a you. Look where it's gotten you. At least I got my rocks off mightily. What do you have to show for it? (BURPS) Yes, that I want to do, strangely enough.

NORA: Okay. List everyone you resent.

MICHAEL: I don't really resent anyone since I'm smarter than everyone.

NORA: What about your mother and father?

MICHAEL: Mama scissorhands? Yes, I guess so.

NORA: And your father?

MICHAEL: I don't remember much about him. You will tell me that he was the real problem. I do remember he drank beer and watched football as I screamed, *Papa, Papa!* while Mom was doing whatever she did, but it's all pretty hazy. I don't have any real memories, just a few flashes here and there, mostly just dispatch … did patch … disPASSionate words. I know some things happened, but it doesn't register.

NORA: You have cut yourself off from the emotions you felt, like you have cut yourself off from your kind and compassionate alter ego. You will flip out if you fully connect. I don't know what you would do, whom you would kill if you recovered these memories. You will not be able to integrate them yourself, any more than you can integrate the horror of what you did to those young girls.

MICHAEL: (SOBER NOW) That's why I need you, Nora.
NORA: No way. I'm not qualified. Bust us out of here and turn yourself in—it's the only way. You will probably die of a heart attack when you abreact.
MICHAEL: And you, somehow, wouldn't want that, despite everything I've done.
NORA: I honestly don't know, Michael. It would save a lot of lives.
MICHAEL. But you don't want me to die, I sense that. Why?
NORA: Don't ask me, Michael. I tell you, I really don't know.
MICHAEL: Yes, you do. It's the "Thou shalt not kill thing, isn't it?" You believe that literally. That's why you won't use your gun even though that beast Bost is planning to kill you even as we speak. He wants to be your bodyguard so that he can kill you. He works for your parents and Ouspensky.
NORA: How do you know that?
MICHAEL: I have my ways. He will rape you first, per his m.o., and then strangle you until your eyes bulge, which he will then eat, an appetizer before he cuts out and eats the main course, your cunt. Which, frankly, I would like to do myself. Don't worry, I'll cut him off myself before he touches a hair on your head. [PENSIVE] And yes, resentments against my father, and every teacher I have ever had and the fucking mediocrity for not stopping me from doing what I do and for thinking he's such a nice guy.
NORA: OK. Now we have to take a little time. Make a sex inventory; write down everyone you have harmed.

DO THIS, DO THIS, DO THIS, DO THIS! Ouspensky interrupted, raging at the acoustic quantum gravity controls of his YouSuck machine.
"No, you fucking jerk, I want to do THIS! Free will, Genya," Nora said patiently, "the ultimate in space-time guidance."

Nora is taken to the Crematorium. Nora is savvy to Ouspensky's tricks now, is not confused by the quark field, navigates it and points out features of the Crematorium to the FBI and CIA via her phone. Michael punches his way off the Braunulan ship and turns himself in and leads ANDREW and a group of detectives to the Doll House.
The detectives and CIA shrinks and cops in riot gear stand paralyzed as they watch Michael abreact. Michael is cuffed and in a straightjacket with manacles on his feet; with an ungodly roar, he tears his way out of the restraints; blood pours out from his ankles where the manacles, now busted, still hang. He is mad and tormented beyond hell.
He looks around at the dead girls in the Doll House with horror, runs to several to give mouth-to-mouth resuscitation and CPR. He blows off the approaching cops with a wave of a superhumanly strong, hyperadrenalized hand. Throughout the abreaction, he begs the cops to kill him and screams "God, what have I done?" Finally, he grabs a cop's gun, sticks it up the roof of his mouth and shoots.
NORA, ESCAPING THE CREMATORIUM, ENTERS AS MICHAEL SHOOTS.
PLEASE, GOD, NORA THINKS.
NORA: Is he dead?

ANDREW NODS YES.
OUSPENSKY chortles, gleeful at the sight of the Doll House and Michael defeated. "Fuck your free will!" he cackles.
ANDREW and others put MICHAEL's lifeless form on a stretcher. Ouspensky comes in with a posse of thugs and grabs Nora. They seize Andrew, too.
NORA: THY WILL, NOT MINE BE DONE. And I am not talking to you, Genya.

Nora sees them club and beat Andrew. Is he dead? No, I would know. They have him surrounded, manacled. Nora is taken back to her apartment, where Bost winks at her. Foe or friend? Nora cannot shake her intuition that he is a friend, despite what Michael and Andrew think.
Andrew, think loud. What is Bost thinking? What is Bost doing? Here, here, think here, zero, hero?
Andrew overhears Zero is coming for me and tears out of his chains. The orcs have never seen anything like it. He overpowers a dozen of their armed stooges, throws Ouspensky aside like a rag, and is coming for me coming for me unstoppable like a bison, a rogue elephant, ready to fight and kill anyone who comes between him and his mate. Come Andrew I am waiting he is roaring he is unstoppable he is running like an animal to come to me down the streets through traffic cars and trucks screech and stop to let him pass he is on the rooftops jumping from one roof to the other he is coming he is coming he is here here hero and takes me away from all of this hey this damsel in distress thing really turns them on … subconscious hostility that they want me to be harmed?

Nora hears Michael's voice as Andrew and an army of cops sweep her to a safe house.
MICHAEL: And, me, dead man walking? And me?
ANDREW: Nora, he's not dead. It's a miracle; the bullet didn't seem to hurt him. We x-rayed and it's just lodged there in his brain. The bullet didn't stop him. He did go into shock, but not before he opened a vein in his right arm and smashed his head against the wall.
NORA: He's alive?
ANDREW: I never saw a man bleed or puke so much. He finally passed out after four hours. He's in the hospital now, conscious; he's stopped trying to kill himself. He just stares at his hands. We have him in a metal mask so he can't bite himself any more. Look.
ANDREW TURNS ON A MONITOR; WE SEE MICHAEL IN A HANNIBAL MASK, CUFFED AND IN FULL RESTRAINT, LYING VERY STILL.
NORA: He can get out of anything you put him in.
ANDREW: We know. But he seems to be staying put.
NORA: I want to talk to him
ANDREW: No. No way. It's too dangerous.
NORA: He can't hurt me now.
ANDREW: We don't know that. No.
NORA: Andrew, he may give me the names of the victims now. Think of that.
ANDREW: I said no.
NORA: What about his rehabilitation, his talent? He could help us.
ANDREW: Remember Norman Mailer and *The Belly of the Beast*? He championed a sociopath's literary career; the perp got paroled and committed another horrible crime.

VOICE OVER THE INTERCOM: Frank, we need the victim's names. Volkhonsky, this is Quantico. We would like you to talk to him. You'll be in another building surrounded by snipers and our best operatives will be in the building with you. Get the names of the victims. We only know six. He might give them to you now. And he said he wants to see you. And by the way, Zero is one of our snipers. She's cool; Bost is the one who's coming for you,

NORA: Thanks, Q.

NORA IS LED BY SNIPERS AND OPERATIVES TO THE SECURE BUILDING. MICHAEL ON A HUGE SCREEN. HE IS ON THE BED, HIS TALL FRAME THIN AND CURVED WITH PAIN. DESPITE THE DISTANCE, HE SENSES NORA'S GAZE IMMEDIATELY. WHAT PASSES FOR HOPE FLASHES IN HIS EYES. HE IS NOW NOT MAD MICHAEL, NOT MIKEY PIECES, OR THE GENIAL JERSEY BOY, BUT ALL OF THEM. ALL ARE ALERT WITH AGONY.

MICHAEL: Nora, I know you love me, so please, please kill me. I am wimping out; I can't seem to do it myself.

NORA (TOUCHED): Michael—you are sorry for what you have done, right? I know you are....

MICHAEL'S EYES CLOSE. WHEN THEY OPEN, WE SEE THE WHOLE AUGUSTUS SMITH FOR THE FIRST TIME, THE KIND PHOTOGRAPHER, THE BOY AND THE MAD GENIUS TOGETHER AS ONE.

NORA: Hello, Gus.

MICHAEL (WAVING HIS IV-TUBED ARM): Call me Michael.

NORA: Mourning, Michael—this is called mourning. And repentance.

MICHAEL: This is beyond … (He dry-heaves a few times.) Beyond …

NORA: Michael, you are sorry? You would never do it again?

MICHAEL'S WILD EYES FOLLOW HER WITH UNBELIEF.

MICHAEL: (SCREAMS) I WILL ALWAYS WANT TO! (CHOKES, COUGHS, SPITS UP. QUIETLY.) This is what I always wanted, for you to forgive me. But I can't forgive myself. Please, Nora, put a pillow over my head. I won't struggle,

NORA: (REGROUPING) Michael, listen—you are powerless over rape and murder and your life has become unmanageable. You agree now, right?

MICHAEL STARES WITH DEAD EYES, THEN NODS.

NORA: There is One who can remove the obsession. Who can remove it, Michael.

MICHAEL: It's not possible.…

NORA (INTERRUPTS): Are you willing to believe in a Power greater than yourself?

MICHAEL (LAUGHS WEAKLY) The shit on the floor is greater than me.

NORA: Michael, it is forgiveness of all sins, *all* sins, or it's all bullshit. And it's not bullshit. Trust God, Michael. God has already forgiven you, seeing you now. Believe that. Clean house so you can forgive yourself. Give me the names of the victims.

MICHAEL: Nora, I kept a detailed list. I'm a sex addict; you know we do that. All the girls. (MICHAEL STARTS TO VOMIT BLOOD; STOPS WITH EFFORT) I can do this; I will do this. (PURE WILL ANIMATES MICHAEL'S PALE FACE) Most of the girls are in the Doll House. If

you look at the back of their costumes, you will find a label with their ... oh God. God ... number, God, and their doll names and real names and everything I did to them. The ones I thought were too ugly are all buried in Manhattan, beneath the basement of FAO Schwartz across the street from the Plaza. They are labeled, too.
NORA: How did you...?
MICHAEL: Christ, Nora, I thought it was funny. Funny. Fucking kill me now. (HOPE FLASHES ACROSS HIS FACE.) I won't eat or drink. I'll tear out the tubes. I CAN do that.
NORA: You can't. You need to make amends to the families.
MICHAEL: How can that be possible? That's not possible. Wait—one of them will kill me! I'll do it, I'll tell them every gory detail, anything not to feel this way.
NORA: Some may forgive you, Michael.
MICHAEL'S FRONT TEETH FALL OUT. NORA REALIZES THE VIOLENCE OF EMOTION HE IS EXPERIENCING.
NORA: We'll talk later. Michael, I swear to you, I know this better than I know anything in the world, it is forgiveness of all sins, *all* sins, or it is all bullshit. And it's not bullshit. If it's good enough for God, you'll do it, too. It will take time, but Michael, you are being called on to save the world, the universe, in fact. That will go a long way toward making amends.
MICHAEL: (DISTASTEFULLY) I was being smart. Clever. Brilliant. Damn me to hell, and I have been, Nora. I will feel this way forever; I suppose it is only fair.
NORA (PRESSING): No, you won't, Michael. You will feel

Love, which, my friend—you are my best friend, weirdly enough—you've never felt before.
MICHAEL: Nora, I still want to kill you.
NORA: I know. Trust God, Michael. This will pass.
MICHAEL: I guess I am going to put on my big boy pants and suck this all up. Not kill myself. Just feel the guilt and remorse.
NORA: Not useful emotions. Think of the service you could do the world. Helping them track down Bost, for example.
MICHAEL: Bost split when he realized you suspected him. He is undercover—or not—in Argentina at a conference of neo-Nazis. He's representing the Bundt region of Pennsylvania. Give me a tough one.
NORA: Deal?
MICHAEL: Returned to the remnants of his lab in Mexico, like a homing pigeon.
NORA: Okay, Ouspensky.
MICHAEL: I have ideas.
NORA: Good, I'll be back.
ANDREW CUTS OFF COMMUNICATION; NORA STOPS HIM.
MICHAEL SMILES. NORA REALIZES THAT, REMORSE NOTWITHSTANDING, MICHAEL WAS IMAGINING HER DEAD, SKINNED BODY DRESSED AS A RUSSIAN PRINCESS AND WAS GETTING AN ERECTION.
MICHAEL: It may never go away.
NORA: You may want to but you don't have to.
MICHAEL: (SMILING WANLY) That is a gift.
NORA POWERS OFF THE VIDEO SCREEN.
MICHAEL: NOW DO THIS! The quark field appears and Michael escapes from FBI and CIA custody.

MICHAEL (STEALING A MERCEDES ON THE STREET): Hey, Nora!!!! I'm going to clean your house! MICHAEL finds THE HOWARD in a luxury glass elevator in his New York City home. MICHAEL sends a flood of hundred-dollar bills through the skylight in the elevator ceiling and THE HOWARD suffocates in money. He drops his collection of pillbox hats on USSASIS, smothering him in smart pink cloth.
PATTI SMITH'S and JOHN LENNON'S reputations are restored.
PATTI SMITH: Don't party with ungroovy people.

***

DO THIS: *NORA accompanies MICHAEL to Deal's lab in Mexico. OUSPENSKY has poisoned the doctor. A dying DEAL tells NORA that she carries the serial killer gene—that he has used her eggs as a cult breeder well beyond the time in the Chalet. She is a breeder of sociopaths and the Mendelian odds are that more than half her children will get the SK chromosome.*
DEAL: (GLOATING THROUGH HIS DEATH RATTLE) We have harvested your eggs and cloned them. We hatched thousands of them, tens of thousands. You, my little saint, are the Typhoid Mary of rape and murder. You have unleashed a plague upon this Earth.
MICHAEL dispatches him and places him on the lab table meant for Nora, one that will resuscitate him and torture him and kill him and revive him and torture him anew. NORA shakes her head *no*, and MICHAEL destroys the table.

DO THIS (OUSPENSKY): *The prince spreads the word throughout major media about sex addict NORA, the Typhoid Mary mother of serial killers.*

DO THIS (NORA): *NORA is now a pariah, like MICHAEL, but they team up to stop the army of serial killers, helping detectives all over the world. One of the first they encounter is NORA'S son CHARLIE, a redneck with missing front teeth and a Confederate flag tattooed on his right arm. He grins toothlessly.*

CHARLIE: Hey, Mom! In a minute, Ah'm gonna be the baddest motherfucker you ever seen, really! C'mon over heah.

MICHAEL QUICKLY SLITS HIS THROAT WITH A SCALPEL.

NORA: Give me the scalpel, Michael. (MICHAEL GIVES IT TO HER.) That was my son. He looks a little like Ouspensky.

MICHAEL: That's why I killed him.

NORA: Not to protect me?

MICHAEL: Always to protect you, serve you. But also, because he looked like Ouspensky. You forgive me?

NORA (KISSES MICHAEL ON THE LIPS). All day long, Michael. All day long.

MICHAEL (THE MURDERER OF THOUSANDS BLUSHES CRIMSON RED. STUTTERS): I never felt anything like that before. Is that how friends kiss?

NORA: Yes. Now I'm going to show you a few other things that friends can do.

MICHAEL: Friends do that?
NORA: Yes, Michael, Gus, Shlomo, whatever your name is. It's called marriage.
MICHAEL: What … I'm stuttering, Nora. What are you saying?
NORA: Don't make me do all the work here, Michael.
MICHAEL: Well, I can provide for you. I have my own island and that building in Tudor City and I own a chain of international hotels and rental apartment buildings. I am rather wealthy from photographic and biomedical patents, including my design of that scalpel, which is popular among plastic surgeons. The scalpel I offed Ouspensky Jr. and Deal with. I have more money than Ouspensky, dear.
NORA: You have to give that to the victims' families.
MICHAEL: I know. But can we keep the island?
NORA: I … no. The island goes, too. We're going to be poor, dear heart. It's not so bad.
MICHAEL: But when I want to kill you?
NORA: Oh, you'll want to kill me. And I'll want to kill you. But it will be different; you'll be my husband.
MICHAEL: Husband—all my life …
NORA (KISSES HIM PASSIONATELY): Later. Come with me. I'd make a pretty hot Rockette, doncha think? Where is your island, anyway?

DO THIS (OUSPENSKY): LEDA, brought back to Frankensteinian life by Dr. Paula Hawk, now leads an army of serial killers. Their brains are programmed by Hawk to hunt for and kill Nora.
LEDA (TAKEN PRISONER BY MICHAEL AND BROUGHT TO NORA): *Dotsinka*, I am your 92-year-old

mother. 92, mother. Old, ancient, sick Mama. I only was undercover with Ouspensky, I played him false for you. I guarded from him the secret of your birth as long as I could. I ask, Tsaritsa Larissa Nikolayevna Romanova, your forgiveness; I cross you and bless Michael. I am not a good Christian, that is to say, I could never forgive anyone who harmed my children.

NORA: Guess there isn't much hope for self-forgiveness.

LEDA STARES WITH HER FACE CONTORTED INTO AN "I'LL GET YOU, YOU BRAT" EXPRESSION.

Nora remembered Leda's bedroom, with small stuffed animals all around her, positioned as though they were fucking, barren otherwise except for a small icon at the top corner of the southeast walls. She remembered the faux treasure chests, hoarding cheap and ugly jewelry.

NORA: May I ask you something, Mama, the swan story, was that a lie? That I saw the black swan approaching the prima while watching *Swan Lake* and yelled, look out, Swan, he's after you! A black swan, like Ouspensky? Was this an implanted screen memory? Did they use me for rituals as a child?

LEDA (PUFFING OUT HER CHEST AND SHAKING HER HEAD VIOLENTLY): But a mother's love is greater than any in the world. . .

Nora heard the voice of one anguished child say, "When the pain got too great I would take them into myself, those who could not endure the pain." Nora went with her to the bones in the mass graves at Kalinivka, sensing her parent's cells there among the flowers and clover growing on the green mounds.

Nora interrupted her own train of thought. "Go with God, Mama. Bless me."

OUSPENSKY (APPEARS IN A PUFF OF SMOKE, LOOKING YOUNGER AND HANDSOMER THAN EVER. TO NORA): The serials are Deal's and Leda's. *You* have no SK genes; all your children join the Peace Corps and such nonsense. Now, accept your throne and me as your royal consort, Larissa Ekaterina Anastasia Nikolayevna Romanova, heir to the throne of all of Russia. Join me and we will depose the *Puto*.
The BIRDS surround NORA, under orders from MICHAEL.
MICHAEL: Yes, *I'M* the one who was working undercover. And we all knew you would fall for these disgusting intergalactic Nazi pigeons.
LEDA cackles.
MICHAEL: Okay, bitch, I've waited long enough. Now I get mine. I am going to kill you, fuck you, and make you my Tsaritsa doll. Ouspensky will give you a Frankenstein brain after I'm done.
BIRDS caw in union, they sound gleeful.
NORA drops MICHAEL with a blow to his neck, takes his scalpel out of her pocket, and calmly slits his throat.
Nora surveyed her handiwork. "It's okay to lie to protect yourself from a predator. And kill."
Planes; sound of artillery fire from the ground; BIRDS shit on New York and fly away.

DO THIS (MICHAEL)

The resurrected monster Michael tracks Ouspensky to a Satanic mass and kills him and throws his corpse on the Walpurgisnacht pyre, to the delight of the guests. Just before committing suicide.

DO THIS (OUSPENSKY)

Coming to his better self, resurrected Michael realizes that Andrew loves Nora more than he does, heads for Cygnus with the Birds, who really are little Nazis. Founds a planet called Pupae. Spends the rest of his life in service to the Nazis, abreacting them, healing them and himself. Says goodbye to Nora with caritas, wants the best for her more than he wants to possess her.

DO THIS (NORA): NO FUCKING WAY. THAT MONSTROUS CREEP MICHAEL IS DEAD AND STAYS DEAD.

DO THIS (ANDREW)

ZERO carries Nora to New York harbor. There we see Audrey Uhuru at the head of an army funded by Baron Bensinck, his huge yacht armed to save the planet. Aura Shevchenko has compiled a dictionary of Braunulan; the ten spaceships have departed. Andrew is waving frantically from the yacht.

Nora grinned. “It’s about time you got here,”

Andrew offered her his hand. Nora got up and dusted herself off.

“Thank you for the REM code.”

“You knew it wasn’t Michael?”

“Fucking woman-hating scum,” Nora replied.

Andrew paused. "Friendship?" he asked tentatively.

Yes, Nora nodded.

Andrew's face lit up. "Sex?" he inquired hopefully.

"Hell, yes," Nora replied. "But I'm tired of Vronsky-Anna. I want Kitty-Levin.

"This isn't a script?" Andrew asked carefully.

Nora smiled. "No way."

"Marriage?" The two stared at each other, lost in smiles.

"Definitely!" Nora answered.

As they walk away together, we hear what sounds like the voice of Johnny Depp. Nora is saying, *baby, am I going too fast for you?*

I am not missing my chance here, Audrey's soul screamed. She raced to the happy couple. "Love is not a feeling you are overwhelmed by; it is a calm, thoughtful decision, a commitment," she said, catching her breath from the run. "You two don't even know each other. Take your time, Nora, you've been through a lot. And you are a Tsaritsa now, think about that."

Bensinck was close behind Audrey. "The CIA is run like the Mafia, dearest Nora. It's really unpleasant. And your consort should be a royal, you know."

"So, you knew Ouspensky was shitting about the Dalai Lama?" Andrew asked.

Nora nodded yes.

"There's a lot you haven't told anyone."

"I told Bost a lot."

"Nora, Andrew never needed Bost!" Audrey turned on Andrew. "Every bit of intel he gave you you could have gotten from someone else. The particle physics?

Why didn't you ask Shevchenko? She's the fucking Nobel laureate, not Bost. He's a fucking rapist."

Ouspensky appeared again in a cloud of smoke, which left dust all over his suit. "As my namesake explored the 4th dimension, I will explore the 17th multiverse," he yelled. "But first, planet Earth."

"Oh, we forgot about you." Nora slipped Andrew's gun away from him and drilled a hole in Ouspensky's forehead.

Ouspensky didn't blink. "You didn't think it would be that easy?" he smiled. The warlock disappeared.

"*C'est à nous, Genya,*" Nora whispered. "*C'est à nous.* She concentrated and the quark field appeared. DO THIS, she commanded space-time.

With Bensinck, Bost experiences male friendship for the first time. They go undercover to track Ouspensky, attend a ritual at 72nd Street in New York; Bensinck shows Bost the Satanic markings on the street, distorted Greek letters like a fraternity. Nothing.

Aura Shevchenko, noble laureate for particle physics, provides the formulae to neutralize the particle accelerator reactions and, with Bensinck, ends the reverse Big Bang.

Nora makes several attempts to reform Bost in space-time. Space-time refuses. Bost is a sociopath, unrepentant, sexist, and cannot believe Shevchenko is smarter than him, even though he has plagiarized her work.

"There is a crack in his psychopathology," Nora tells

the quark field. "Friendship for me, Bensinck. This is not a homogeneous sociopath; there is good there."

SPACE-TIME: OF COURSE NOT HOMOGENOUS, ALWAYS A DAPPLE OR STRIPE OF GOOD. BUT HE IS SMELLY. LET ME DEAL WITH HIM.

DO THIS (BOST)

Bost, returned from South America, picks off the CIA and FBI agents from the window of Nora's apartment for fun. A double agent working for Ouspensky, he has a sudden spiritual awakening. He realizes Nora genuinely loved him and may have wanted to have his baby.

DO THIS (NORA)

Well, I tried. Baby? I don't think so. Empathy 101, Bostie. You are a severe clinical narcissist and are missing a range of human capabilities, empathy, genuine self-examination, the ability to learn from mistakes since you lack the ego-strength to accept that you can make them. You're fucked, Neils.

DO THIS (OUSPENSKY)

As Nora remembers and processes her relationship to Ouspensky, she becomes insane. She thinks she makes the trees, her pets, move in the wind. She talks to a branch shaped like the face of a wise Ent. We see her dancing on the spray-painted red Greek letters on the tarmac in front of Ouspensky's townhouse, where a Black Mass is in full throttle. Nora feels magnetically compelled to enter the townhouse to see Ouspensky again, her love addiction qualifier.

DO THIS (ANDREW)

Nora forces herself away and runs to Riverside Park to the statue of Eleanor Roosevelt at the entrance, a patron saint of hers; Andrew joins her. Andrew offers friendship and ice skating but does not want to have sex until she does her SLAA 9th step.

"That could take years," she exclaims.

"I can wait."

She agrees. "You're getting the hang of this."

DO THIS (NORA)

Ouspensky finds that all his malefactor allies have flown. Outside of the Vienna Opera House, he has a complete nervous breakdown, suddenly breaking into weird uga chooga *noises from Pink Floyd songs. He causes a major distraction and is arrested.*

Thank you, space-time. That will be all. Except, I don't believe, Nora posited, that the standard model has actually been unified with gravity, nor in quantum gravity and the theory of everything. The strong force and gravity are alike because they deal with mass, the electroweak and electromagnetism deal with electrons, that's how you unify field theory for those two quadrants. Gravitons are different than electrons, two fundamentally different forces, yes? Why unify it just because it is there? And acoustic space-time? Well, just look at it, can we? One more thing, dear ST: We women will never forget. Those who do not remember history, as those of us who have been drugged and tormented and raped and pissed on and STILL REMEMBER … I don't even have words for the contempt I have for you predators.

Arrested, Ouspensky tells the cops that he taught Nora face. Sitting on his face, cunnilingus by "Because the Night" by Patti Smith.

"He taught me nothing," Nora tells the cops. "Don't party with ungroovy people.

Copy Cat

For Michael, Neils Bost and Prince Eugene Ouspensky

You know, the last time I worked like a working girl
Satan he comes to my house
I mean visits he's one of those boys who
can't come unless he kills someone
so
he strips
takes his clothing off
takes the uniform
the badge the boots the trooper uniform off
his little Hitler mustache is all he's got on
and I say sipping scotch — oh my there look at your wee
wee
Satan say honey don't be talking baby talk
what you see here is my prick
and I say not so kindly I'm a little drunk I say:
Satan baby
officer mine
I hate to inform you
hesitate to inform you
wouldn't dare to inform on you
but Satan
I've seen plenty of pricks
miles of cock
piles of penises
and Satan
what you got there
is a wee wee.

a hot dog (not)
a mean love muscle (I don't think so)
a throbbing cock?
well no
not until you get me in your arms and pin me down
beat my face
slam the bottle up my cunt
fuck my ass until it bleeds
then yer a brick house

when you see blood yer pretty hot
and I say
call the police
but yer already there

since I'm going to die
come on baby
let's have a date
we can talk some more
I know you love to talk and stalk

look watch:
watch me through my window
I know you're there
little man
I see you
and I don't care

you don't exist
you're just a wannabe in a uniform
I stand naked in the window

mocking you every night
you dream of dismembering me
you want to push my face
my laughing mocking face
so far down into the ground
you can't see anything
no eyes no laughing mouth
just the back of my pretty head
like a pumpkin
ready to smash you want to
push me down into the ground make me eat gravel
make me eat dirt make me eat my laughing mocking words

saying no no
not you
everybody else
anybody else
but not you

you want to
shut my big laughing mouth
throw me to the ground dance on my back till it breaks
till it bleeds

you want to wipe
the smile and the lipstick off my face
put blood where the red paint is

you
like it like that

my butt is yours just for just one night
as long as you're holding that shiny knife

oh baby
I call the police and there you are
cop cop copy cat
but you can't dance and you can't come and you can't
even move your gun
unless you see the fear and scum
do you kill young boys
cause you can't get it up
do you kill young girls cause you can't get enough

georgy porgy pudding and pie
kiss the girls
kiss the girls
kiss the girls
kiss the girls
kiss the girls
kiss the girls
kiss the girls
kiss the girls
can't come unless they run can't come until they run
can't come until they run
until they twist and shout

how many will you have to kill to
shut my laughing mocking mouth
red with lipstick
wet with

other men's come
how many will you have to kill
to make me want you
notice you
remember you're alive?
how much attention do you want how much attention do you need you ain't never gonna get my undying undying undying attention

that's the way you like it
me
face
down
no longer even
screaming moving
only the twitching of my dying limbs only that warm soft blood like the animals you killed when you were small mama said they were going to God and you just helped and now you see the inside of me I'm losing blood I'm fast asleep so peaceful now you feel the love I feel for you we're finally one I'm going soon and we are one how much how much how much love

and now finally I understand and darling
I'll never laugh at you again mock you point to your tiny itsy bitsy penis
your tiny little-boy penis and laugh saying

You
ain't never gonna be no man
I'm your mama

and baby I know
watch me little boy I'll undress for you pull you over
let you
come to mama
be with mama
come watch mama
little boy

but yer
too little
too little
so
I go
with the men
you
just watch
and I'll laugh and my lovers and everyone else
will laugh at you
and how you will love me
till the day I die
especially on the day I die

come on push my face down into the ground you'll be
my dad
and I'll
finally
be
your mom

Nora leafed through her papers. "Oh, yes and I wrote a story, 'Heat,' in which the female protagonist comes to orgasm strangling Ouspensky as he is raping her.

He starts fucking her with his tiny dick and Nora starts fantasizing about killing him and it turns her on. She puts her hands around his skinny neck and squeezes and this makes Ouspensky hotter. He is going to come and Nora squeezes tighter and he comes and gasps. As his body shudders in its final death rattle, Nora comes volcanically, throwing Ouspensky's corpse out of her body with the force of her climax.

Bensinck hugged Nora. He wrote on a piece of paper, which he pushed toward her: *Sex, friendship, and Kitty-Levin. And a good deal of money, my impoverished Tsaritsa,* it read.

Nora smiled. "All these years …"

Bensinck dropped to one knee and took her hand. "No more undercover, no more faking it. Just us, and a quarter of the world's land mass. We have a war to fight. Shall we do this, finally, together?

Nora smiled. "And create a world safe for our children, Albert? Or am I going too fast for you?"

FIN

APPENDIX:
NORA'S SLAA SEXUAL HARMS INVENTORY (FRAGMENT)

Sexual Ideal

I have sex with a man whom I love and respect and trust and am attracted to and who loves and respects and trusts me and is attracted to me as part of a committed relationship and as a byproduct of sharing and partnership. Our sex is creative, playful, imaginative, and hot.

[following pages illegible]

Glenn

Reason for getting involved

He was tall

Specific sex conduct

Played him off of Steve and Stuart

Major points that came up

He told me that I couldn't whore around and have a steady boyfriend and I dumped him. I didn't have much concern for his feelings. He reached out to me later and I ignored his concern. He was real about my problems and I was in denial.

Where have I been dishonest?

Getting involved with someone I didn't care for

Where have I been inconsiderate?

Playing him.

Whom did I hurt? (Look beyond the relationship)

Stuart and Steve

Did I arouse jealousy?

I don't know, I wasn't paying enough attention.

Did I arouse bitterness?

Yes, obviously; he wanted me to be faithful.

What should I have done instead?

Not be a fucking sex addict.

Include specific harms

He came to see me and I threw him out based on one remark.

Stuart

Motives for getting involved

Wanted a boyfriend [text illegible] He said another girl was his dream and that I was the "reality" and I still fucked him. But hated him for it and got revenge later. I "made him" fall in love with me two years later when I was on top of the world, was seductive because male attention and getting men to fall in love with me was my game, even though I was not serious about him. But it was very satisfying to have him under my thumb.

Where have I been selfish?

Toyed with his affections because I liked being admired and having sexual power over men. Dismissed him without apology.

Whom did I hurt? (Look beyond the relationship)

Glenn; ran to Peter with this situation and used it to manipulate him.

Did I arouse bitterness?

Yes, Stuart felt I had set this whole thing up.

Where was I at fault?

Liked playing with men's feelings, having them love and admire me

What should I have done instead?

Avoided hurting people who cared for me.

Armando

Motives for getting involved

He was very wealthy

Specific sex conduct

Dumped him summarily which made him hysterical. Loving that someone "loved" me enough to be in agony when I broke up with him. Enjoyed the fact that he was hurt because it meant I had power and impact. I need to seek other ways of expressing power and impact.

[text illegible; missing pages]

Include specific harms

To self, to precious self.

Hans

Motives for getting involved

Needed a friend and he was one.

Specific sex conduct

Infidelity, sexual shaming.

Major points that came up

He was the best friend I ever had and I treated him like dirt. Was unfaithful to him and pissed when he wouldn't forgive me fast enough. Took money from him to support a lover. Expected him to protect, rescue. and help me no matter what I did. Became a poet and excluded him from my readings because I wanted to fuck and intrigue with the men there.

How did it end?

He finally became disgusted with me.

Where have I been selfish?

This relationship was all about me, my needs, my "recovery," my drama and trauma. He was a far distant second. His needs were pretty much unimportant to me.

Where have I been dishonest?

Infidelity. I was "honest" about that to relieve my guilt.

Did I arouse jealousy?

Yes. I would dress up for SLAA meetings in order to intrigue.

[illegible—page 174] **bitterness?**

. . . power. He ate rice and beans while supporting me and Ouspensky. Used him.

Jesse

Cheated on him, used him, disrespected him as a man. Took comfort, love. and support from him and gave none back. Threw him away when I was done. Literally threw him out because, revolving door style, I had another lover coming to fuck.

How did it end?

With him hating me.

Where have I been selfish?

Where wasn't I? Enjoyed his being in love with me and toyed with him.

Where have I been dishonest?

Gave him to believe I cared more than I did.

[missing pages—page 378]

Major points that came up

He tolerated my dysfunction.

How did it end?

Still kinda friends, with me looking down upon him.

[page 600] I could abuse him and he would keep coming back. Shock and jealousy when he stopped loving me and fell in love with Lisa.

John W.

Motives for getting involved

He was cool and a rebel and an artist.

Specific sex conduct

Helped to break up his relationship with his male lover; told him I was a prostitute to seduce him. Paid his bills and gave him spending money to keep him.

Major points that came up

Blamed him for Russell's murder without proof. Violence and horrible arguments. I was insane; he slept with men.

How did it end?

In an ugly, insane way.

Where have I been selfish?

Blamed my promiscuity on him. Was obsessed with him

Did I arouse jealousy?

Yes, John was upset when I slept with Prince Andrei.

Did I arouse bitterness?

I was a destructive force in this relationship, insane, starting fires, inciting rage and vengeance.

Where was I at fault?

I was drinking, drugging, encouraging dangerous and hateful behavior.

What should I have done instead? Include specific harms

Been a different person.

Prince Andrei

Motives for getting involved

He was rich and handsome and I wanted to get back at John for sleeping with boys

Specific sex conduct

Broke up his relationship with Edith without being really sure I wanted to commit to him; used him as an escape from John, until I went back to him. Enjoyed our sex life.

Major points that came up

Screamed at him and abused him constantly. Made invidious comparisons to John. Looked down upon him when he was depressed. Thought he was less than because he inherited his wealth and did not earn it. Looked down upon him intellectually. Was not grateful for the rescue from my sordid life, the beauty of Mexico he exposed me to, his affection, and the opportunity he gave me to be an artist.

How did it end?

My leaving him to chase John, my obsession, soon to be displaced by Ouspensky.

Where have I been selfish?

Throughout. Used him to pay for my friend's tabs, used him

DADA Professor

Motives for getting involved

He seemed to want sex; like the cabdriver I slept with who seemed to want to have sex who was appalled by the degradation of our backseat fuck.

[missing pages] Got gonorrhea and gave it to Prince Andrei and who knows how many men.

How did it end?

Here ends the sex inventory fragment of her serene highness Tsaritsa Larissa Ekaterina Anastasia Nikolayevna Romanova.

Larissa Shmailo is a poet, novelist, translator, editor, anthologist, and critic. Her poetry collections are *Medusa's Country*, *#specialcharacters*, *In Paran*, the chapbook *A Cure for Suicide*, and the e-book *Fib Sequence;* her debut novel was *Patient Women*. Shmailo's poetry CDs are *The No-Net World* and *Exorcism*, available through Spotify, Amazon, iTunes, Deezer, and other digital distributors. Shmailo's work has appeared in *Plume*, the *Brooklyn Rail*, *Fulcrum*, the *Journal of Feminist Studies in Religion*, the *Journal of Poetics Research*, *Drunken Boat*, *Barrow Street*, *Gargoyle*, and the anthologies *Measure for Measure: An Anthology of Poetic Meters*, *Words for the Wedding*, *Contemporary Russian Poetry*, *Resist Much/Obey Little: Poems for the Inaugural*, *Verde que te quiero verde: Poems after Garcia Lorca*, and many others.

Shmailo is the original English-language translator of the world's first performance piece, *Victory over the Sun* by Alexei Kruchenych, performed at the Los Angeles County Museum of Art, the Garage Museum of Moscow, the Brooklyn Academy of Art, and theaters and universities worldwide. Shmailo also edited the anthology *Twenty-first Century Russian Poetry* and has been a translator on the Russian Bible for the Eugene A. Nida Institute for Biblical Scholarship of the American Bible Society.

Shmailo's work is in the libraries of Harvard, Princeton, Yale, Stanford, and New York universities, the Hirshhorn Museum of the Smithsonian, the Museum of Modern Art

(MoMA), the New York Museum of Natural History, and other universities and museums. She received honorable mention in the Compass Award for Russian literary translation in 2011, the Elizabeth P. Braddock poetry prize in 2012, and the Goodreads May 2012 poetry contest; she was a finalist in the Glass Woman prose prize in 2012, and a semifinalist in the Subito Press/University of Boulder prose competition. Larissa also received the New Century Music awards for best spoken word with rock, jazz, and electronica in 2009, as well as the best album award for her CD *Exorcism*. She has read at the Knitting Factory, Barnard College, the New School, New York University, the Langston Hughes residence, and for American Express/Share Our Strength.

She blogs at http://larissashmailo.blogspot.com/

Please visit her website at www.larissashmailo.com.

Made in the USA
Lexington, KY
19 January 2019